Grim

The Perished Riders MC - Book 3

Nicola Jane

Copyright © 2022 by Nicola Jane

All rights reserved.

No portion of this book may be reproduced in any form without written permission from the publisher or author, except as permitted by U.K. copyright law.

Meet the team

Cover Designer: Charli Childs, Cosmic Letterz Design
Editor: Rebecca Vazquez – Dark Syde Books
Proofreader: Jackie Ziegler
Formatting: Nicola Miller

Disclaimer:

This book is a work of fiction. The names, characters, places, and incidents are all products of the author's imagination and are not to be construed as real. Any similarities are entirely coincidental.

Spelling Note:

Please note, this author resides in the United Kingdom and is using British English. Therefore, some words may be viewed as incorrect or spelled incorrectly, however, they are not.

Acknowledgements

My team, forever supporting, encouraging, and accepting me into the 'mean girls'. You rock! Here's to the future xx

Contents

A note from the Author	VII
PLAYLIST	VIII
CHAPTER ONE	1
CHAPTER TWO	12
CHAPTER THREE	20
CHAPTER FOUR	31
CHAPTER FIVE	40
CHAPTER SIX	51
CHAPTER SEVEN	62
CHAPTER EIGHT	73
CHAPTER NINE	82
CHAPTER TEN	93
CHAPTER ELEVEN	102
CHAPTER TWELVE	112
CHAPTER THIRTEEN	123
CHAPTER FOURTEEN	131
CHAPTER FIFTEEN	143
CHAPTER SIXTEEN	152

CHAPTER SEVENTEEN	162
CHAPTER EIGHTEEN	171
CHAPTER NINETEEN	181
CHAPTER TWENTY	188
CHAPTER TWENTY-ONE	196
CHAPTER TWENTY-TWO	202
CHAPTER TWENTY-THREE	209
Ghost - The Perished Riders MC	213
1. A note from me to you	224
2. Popular books by Nicola Jane	226

A note from the Author

The material in this book may be viewed as offensive to some readers, including graphic language, sexual situations, murder, and violence. This is mainly because it's an MC romance story and they all tend to contain one or more of the above.

Grim will send you crazy with his terrible behaviour and all complaints should be directed to his President, Maverick.

Happy Reading x

PLAYLIST

By Your Side - Sade
  Still Into You - Paramore
  Anything for You - Gloria Estefan
  lie to me - Tate McRae & Ali Gatie
  Is It Just Me? - Emily Burns ft. JP Cooper
  Truth Be Told - Matthew West ft. Carly Pearce
  Can't Let Go - Adele
  Infatuation - Maroon 5
  Secret - Maroon 5
  Rush - Lewis Capaldi ft. Jessie Reyez
  What I Put You Through - Conor Maynard
  Sometimes Love Just Ain't Enough - Travis Tritt
  Bad Liar - Imagine Dragons
  She Used To Be Mine - Sara Bareilles
  You Lost Me - Christina Aguilera
  Stickwitu -The Pussycat Dolls
  Consequences - Camila Cabello
  We Belong Together - Mariah Carey
  Mr. Wrong - Mary J. Blige ft. Drake
  Take a Bow - Rihanna
  Too Lost in You - Sugababes

CHAPTER ONE

GRIM

Babies. I don't get the fuss. They cry, they smell funny, and they don't do anything apart from eat, shit, and sleep. I've never really been around them, and I don't intend to stick around now as I grab my jacket and head for the door. "Going somewhere?" Meli gives me a sly smile, and I narrow my eyes. "Because I'm pretty certain Mav said everyone needs to be here tonight."

"I'm the VP, I'm exempt." I'm almost out the door.

"Let me just check that with your Pres before you high-tail out of here," she says, smirking as she waves to her brother.

My President, Maverick, heads over with a beer in his hand and a stupid goofy smile on his face. Why do babies make everyone grin like that? "Our first club baby," he says, holding up his beer, and I arch my brow. He takes in my jacket and bike keys, and he tips his head to one side. "What's happened?"

"Nothing," I mutter, irritated that Meli's dropped me in it. She somehow always finds a way to piss me the fuck off.

"I'm thinking there must be a real good reason you're leaving here tonight when I specifically said we were all staying here to celebrate."

"Come on, Mav," I say with a sigh.

"Pres," he corrects me, and I roll my eyes. It's our little thing—he insists I call him Pres, but we've been mates since we were in the womb, so calling him Pres is weird. "Please tell us where else you have to be that's more important than welcoming Scar and Gracie's first child."

I growl, irritated. "The kid's a day old. He don't care."

"I care. It's club duties, you gotta stay," says Mav with a smug smile. Club duties is something he throws at the brothers when he's giving no option but his way.

"Can I point out again," I mutter, laying my jacket back on the chair, "that this is your dream, not mine."

He pats me on the back, laughing. "I got that, but as my VP, your job is to make my dream work. That starts by staying here and celebrating our next generation."

Slumping down near Hadley, I grab the beer Ghost passes me and glance at Mav's younger sister. She's always got her head in a book and it irritates me. "Why don't you do that shit upstairs?" I snap.

"Don't get moody at me because Mav pulled rank," she utters, not bothering to look up from the tatty paperback.

"What are you reading?" asks Ghost, joining me on the couch.

"You wouldn't know it," Hadley mumbles. I reach over, snatching the book, and she glares. "What are we, teenagers?"

Ghost takes it from me, scanning his eyes over the pages before laughing. "Shit, Hads, does this stuff come with an age warning?"

"I read it for the romance," she snaps, her cheeks flushing.

"Like hell you do." He chuckles, arching a brow. "Is this legal? How the hell does he last this long if she's so fucking hot?" he asks, reading with interest.

"Read it, you might learn," says Rosey, joining us.

"Hey, I can last," argues Ghost. "Just with the shit this guy's doing, it's impossible."

"Maybe that's why it's called fiction, because it's not real," says Rosey sarcastically. "Women write it down and call it fiction, but what they really wanna call it is dreams that will never come true."

"Is that why you read it, Hads?" I ask. "You'll only be disappointed when you actually have sex."

"Wow," hisses Rosey, narrowing her eyes in anger.

"I'm just saying, she's getting the wrong idea about relationships. Bet that book doesn't tell you how he'll fuck her friend just as good, maybe her cousin too. He'll probably tell her how amazing she is right before cheating or breaking her heart."

"That's the beauty of it," Hadley says, taking her book back from Ghost. "It's fantasy, better than real life. Maybe if you read more, you wouldn't be such a bitter, resentful arsehole." Everyone around us laughs. I don't. How the hell does she do that, be so calm and cool when she delivers a blow? I don't think I've ever heard her shout or get mad. The closest she came was when Rosey shot her half-brother, but even then, it was mostly tears.

"Better to be an arsehole and live in the real world," I snap, "than a fake character in your book of unachievable dreams."

I wait until the guys begin to disappear. We have a busy day tomorrow helping Arthur Taylor with money collections. The club works alongside the mafia—we help them, they help us, and we all live amongst one another in harmony.

I head out to my bike, throwing my leg over and immediately feeling calm. Something about the road keeps on calling me. I love being here at the club with Mav, but I can't deny my feet are getting itchy to hit the road again. We spent a few years travelling together until Eagle, Mav's old man, died and we returned to The Perished Riders. Then, Maverick was voted in as President and he chose me to be his VP. And that's where our adventure ended . . . or began, if you look at it through Mav's eyes.

Before I know it, I'm stopping outside Mum's place. It's a big house split into small bedsits. The main door is open, cos someone bust the lock weeks ago and the landlord hasn't fixed it. I guess he doesn't see the point as someone will just break it again.

Mum's place is on the ground floor, and when I knock on her door, it swings open. A drunk guy, double my age, staggers out, not noticing me waiting to enter. Stepping inside, I shake my head and sigh. The hall is littered with discarded wrappers and empty beer cans. If I was to dig around, no doubt there'd be used needles too.

To my left is the small kitchenette. It's basic, with a kettle and toaster. She didn't bother to get an oven or microwave because she doesn't eat, and when she does, she gets take-out. Mum is hunched in an old, dirty-looking armchair. Her greasy, matted hair hides her pale face.

I crouch down and whisper, "Ma." A small grunt escapes her. "It's me, Hudson."

She raises her head slightly and peeks out through her hair. Her washed-out complexion only highlights the dark circles under her eyes. "Hudson," she whispers in a croaky voice. I smile, brushing her lank hair from her eyes.

"Hey, Ma. How ya doing?"

"I need—" she mumbles, and I know exactly what she's going to say.

"Some food and sleep," I cut in.

"It hurts, baby," she croaks, starting to rock back and forth. "It hurts."

Her words haunt me, reminding me of when I was a small child, before Dad came and took me away from this hell. It pains me now that he had to die and she's still here, living her life like this. Wasting away.

"I can take the pain away, Ma," I reply, and she almost looks hopeful. "If you come back with me." It's an offer I make every week when I come to see her. She looks crushed, and another muffled noise leaves her throat. "I'm not gonna give you money, Ma. I never do."

Her bony hand reaches for my arm, and she digs her fingers into the leather of my kutte. "You hate me," she whispers, tears filling her eyes. "You hate me so much."

"I don't hate you, Ma. I love you, and that's why I want you to get help."

"They'll come for me," she says.

I sigh. "No one's coming." It's a lie she tells to get money, one that terrified me as a kid. "Do you need food?"

She shakes her head. "I need money, just five pounds."

I stand, and her hand falls away. "I'll come back soon."

"Please," she begs, the tears now rolling down her dirty face. "I need it so badly."

"You need help. When you agree to that, I'll take you back to mine and clean you up. Ma, you're running out of time. I'm gonna come here soon and find your body in that chair. Is that how you wanna go?"

"Hudson, if you love me, you'll get me the money."

"I do love you, and that's exactly why I'm not." I turn and leave.

I get back to the club and grab a beer from the bar. Whenever I've seen her, I feel the urge to get wasted. Skye, one of the club whores, sidles over with a sexy smirk on her face. "You look like you need a friend," she says.

I grab her wrist and tug her to me, and she giggles. "What I need is someone to fuck."

"Ugh, how disgusting," comes Meli's voice from behind the bar.

I release Skye immediately, like I'm doing something wrong. "Why are you behind there?"

"I was cleaning up for Nelly. She had to leave early."

"You shouldn't be sneaking around."

"Off you go then. I'm sure after that smooth line, Skye is desperate to bounce on your cock," she says, laughing to herself.

Meli jumps when I slam my beer down, causing it to spill over the top. "Watch your mouth, Amelia."

"Or you'll wash it out for me?" she whispers, biting her lower lip.

I swallow, my eyes watching the way her teeth graze the soft, plump skin. "Skye, go," I mutter, and she leaves. "What are you playing at?"

Meli arches her perfectly plucked brow. "Me? Nothing. I see you went out even though Mav said you had to stay."

"I had some business to attend to."

"A woman?" she asks, wiping the bar top. I grab her wrist, and she looks into my eyes.

"We said we wouldn't do it again," I remind her.

"I know."

"So why are you trying to entice me?"

"I'm wiping the bar. What's enticing about that?"

I stand, moving around the bar and towards her. "First, you try and stop me leaving tonight, then you cock-block me with Skye . . . what do you want, Meli?" Her head tips back the closer I get, until she's against the wall. "You're playing with fire," I add, glancing around to make sure the area is still empty.

"What can I say, I like the heat," she replies.

My mouth crashes against hers in a desperate kiss. Our teeth clash as I hungrily swipe my tongue against hers. She runs her fingers through my hair, pulling me closer. We suddenly stop, staring at each other with heat in our eyes. Our breathing is laboured, and she smirks. "Not here," she whispers, sliding under my arm and going down the cellar steps.

I follow, cos I'm too weak to say no. I've liked Meli for a long time, and after Mav and I left, I thought that would fade, but seeing her again brought it all back. And then we had one night, one drunken night after Rosey returned and dropped the bombshell about Meli and Ripper and the shit he'd been doing to her. We were both wasted and feeling low, and while my memory is sketchy, I don't regret it. I spent years wanting Meli, and my only regret is I don't remember our one night together very well.

※

I come with such force, my legs go weak and I stumble back from her. Meli glances back over her shoulder, her perfect arse on show, and she grins. "Better?" she asks, and I nod, not trusting myself to speak. "Before the guilt starts, don't worry, my lips are sealed."

No one knows about us, and we like it that way. I'm not sure how Mav would react, he's not as controlling as his dad was, but I'm his VP and he'd hate us sneaking around. She's right—as I fasten my jeans, the guilt does start to creep in. "I gotta go," I mutter.

"I know," she says, shrugging her shoulders. "Goodnight."

HADLEY

I wake earlier than usual and stretch out. I love the weekends when I don't have to rush around and get to work. I pull on my joggers and baggy jumper, and once I've brushed my teeth, I put my hair into a messy bun and grab my book. Most of the guys will still be sleeping, so it'll be nice and quiet.

I make a strong black coffee and head outside and round the back of the clubhouse. It sits on empty land that stretches for miles, over fields of green with a wooded area at the end. I prefer the large oak tree right out back. I used to sit under it a lot as a kid and think my worries away.

I almost turn back, though, when I see my usual spot taken. Grim looks up and his eyes are red, like he's super tired. "Everything okay?" I ask. He sways the beer can hanging loosely in his grip as if to explain why he's sitting here at six in the morning. "I'll go," I mutter, but he shuffles over, making space for me to join him.

Taking a seat on the grass, I lean my back against the rough trunk. We both stare out over the fields in silence. It reminds me of when we were younger. There's around ten years between us, but when I was fourteen, I'd sit here because I knew it was Grim's favourite spot. When he'd turn up drunk or after a hard night, he'd stumble over and sit beside me in silence. I loved it. I savoured every second spent with him, even though he didn't give me a second thought.

Once he left with Mav, I moved on. My stupid teenage crush was forgotten, and although I was never as promiscuous as my twin sister, I dated a couple of guys. But when Grim returned, it was like he'd never left, and that stupid teenager in me did a happy dance. Only now, he's stronger, bigger, and more toned. I secretly watch him from afar, knowing he'll never feel the same about me but wishing that for once, he'd look at me like he looks at my sister.

Grim takes a drink from the can and realises it's empty. He crushes it and drops it to the ground, then pulls a hip flask from his inside jacket pocket and unscrews the cap, offering it to me. I shake my head, and he shrugs, drinking a few mouthfuls and wiping his mouth on the back of his hand. "Don't you have collections today?" I ask.

He groans. "Fuck."

"Maybe put the flask away," I suggest. He hands it to me, and I stare at the engraved emblem of the club's badge. My dad had one exactly the same. "Try this," I say, handing him my coffee. I watch as he takes a sip and screws up his face. "I know, it's really strong, but it's the best."

"It's like treacle," he mutters in disgust, and I laugh.

"I pay to have it shipped in from Colombia. I can't get it here." He scrubs his hands over his tired face. "You should try and sleep," I say, but he gives me a look, telling me it's a dumb statement. "What's bothering you?"

"Aww, Hads, don't try that bullshit on me, it doesn't work."

"Bullshit?"

"That listening thing you do, like you actually give a crap." I'm offended, and it must show on my face. "Sorry, it's just, talking don't do shit. My problems don't melt away because I've said them out loud."

"How would you know?" I ask patiently as he stares at me blankly. "How would you know if it works or not? Have you ever tried talking about things?"

"I don't need to try it to know it doesn't work. Are you gonna save my mum?"

I frown. He didn't mean to mention her and his face shows it instantly. I decide to tread lightly. "Parents can be hard work, especially if they don't want the help." I remember my mum talking about Grim's mum, Carol, in the past. She's an addict, and Grim's dad took custody of him when he was young. "I can't believe she's still around," I add, then wince at how that sounds. "I mean, in your life."

"She isn't," he mutters, handing me the now empty coffee cup and standing. "Don't tell anyone about her, Hads. I like my life to stay private."

"Even from the club?" I ask, arching a brow.

"Especially from the club."

He stomps away and disappears back inside. He's troubled, and I know his mum is the cause of it.

CHAPTER TWO

GRIM

My head is pounding almost as loud as Ghost is banging on this customer's door. "I thought they called you Ghost on account you're quiet, no one sees you coming."

"Yeah," he says, shrugging.

"I don't know when you're ever fucking stealthy," I mutter, rubbing my tired eyes with irritation. "Everything about you is loud. Even the steps you take are like fucking elephants."

Ghost laughs. "Someone got out the wrong side of the bed. Whose bed is the real question."

I glare at him, my thoughts turning to Meli and what we did last night. "Let's not talk for a while, you're getting on my nerves."

The door opens and the guy behind it sighs heavily. "I don't have it."

I groan. "I gave you a week, man."

"It's not long enough."

"I can't go back and tell Mr. Taylor that," I snap. "He'll send me back here to cut your throat."

The guy pales, and I feel for him. He's got small kids and a wife to take care of, and the loan was to help with living costs. Apparently, raising kids isn't cheap these days. "How long do you need?" I ask on a sigh, and he looks hopeful.

"Another week?"

I nod once and turn to leave. Ghost rushes after me. "Are you joking? Arthur will have our nuts."

"Fuck Arthur. I'm not in the mood for this shit today."

Mav is waiting by the bikes, and he looks up as we exit the building. "That was quick. You get the money?"

I shake my head, and his mouth falls open in shock. "Arthur's gonna explode. This guy's taking liberties."

"It makes no sense to me how we help vulnerable women in the community yet we're gonna beat this guy, which will only upset his woman," I argue. "He doesn't have the money, so what the fuck can I do about it? I'm not Arthur's henchman, so if he wants to dish out a beating, let him do it."

"What the hell is wrong with you?" Mav asks. "You've been a moody bastard all day. You know that guy isn't innocent. He used the cash to buy drugs to sell. He should have the cash to pay his debts off."

I throw my leg over my bike. "Then go get it, Mav."

"Pres!" he reminds me. "Go home. You're no fucking use to me today," he mutters.

I ride off without responding. I've got too much on my mind and collecting debts for Arthur fucking Taylor isn't my priority.

Stopping my bike outside the cemetery, I get off and head straight for my old man's grave. Coming here helps—I like the peace it offers. There're fresh roses, no doubt laid by one of the ol' ladies. I know Mama B comes here a lot to sit with Eagle and always lays flowers for him, even though he was a dick. Then, she secretly visits Viper, the club's Vice President back when Mav and I were still kids. When Mav was just ten years old, he was ordered to put a bullet in Viper, after it came to light that he and Brea were having an affair. She also lays flowers for Crow, her and Viper's son. He isn't buried here, instead resting in hell under a fuck load of concrete, but I guess she needs somewhere to pay her respects.

I lower to the damp grass, resting my back against my dad's headstone. "How's it going, old man?" I ask aloud. "I'm having the week from hell, but I guess you already know that, right?" An elderly couple passes, nodding their heads to me in greeting. Once they're out of earshot, I lean my head back and stare up at the blue sky. "If she's gonna die, I wish she'd just go already. I feel like it's a waiting game. Every week, I turn up there and see the same shit. I hold my damn breath when I touch her, expecting to feel her cold and stiff. And if she ain't gonna die, why won't she accept help and get better?"

A magpie calls out as it swoops over and lands on a nearby gravestone. "If that's your sign, it's not enough. I know what you're trying to say. You think I should wash my hands of her, but how can I, Pops?" It was my nickname for him as I got older. "If you were still here, you'd be checking in on her too. She was your ol' lady at one point, and you committed to watching her even when she fucked up. And now, that's passed to me." I sigh heavily. "I hate this worry. It never leaves my chest, Pops."

HADLEY

Faith gives me a worried look as I grab hold of her hand and carefully push the front door open. It was my idea to come here and see if I could talk to Grim's mum, but I'm having doubts now I'm here. I also dragged poor Faith along for the ride because she hardly ever leaves the clubhouse since we helped her through a traumatic time in her life.

Going inside, we find her apartment door open too, and as I step farther in, I pinch my nose. The place stinks and there's discarded belongings everywhere. "I bet there's rats in here," whispers Faith.

"Probably," I agree, noticing food waste littered around the place. There's a guy lying face-down on the kitchen table with a used needle in his hand. "Oh Christ," I mutter.

The next room has a door half hanging from its hinges. Inside is Grim's mum, slumped in a chair, strung out. She looks thinner and more tired than I remember, but I was a little girl last time she was around. She hasn't aged well and her hair is hanging in her face in straggly, greasy clumps. As I step into the room, I notice a guy standing in the corner, emptying dresser drawers onto the floor. He stops, staring wide eyed at me. "I need cash," he snaps, and Faith squeezes my arm in panic.

"I don't have—"

"Now!" he screams, dropping the drawer and moving towards me. I fumble in my bag, pulling out a crumpled banknote. He snatches it without checking the amount and runs out.

"Holy crap, this is a drug den," whispers Faith. I feel bad, cos if I'd have known, I wouldn't have brought her along. She's been through enough.

"Carol," I say, gently. "I'm Hadley, one of Grim's friends." At the mention of Grim, she glances up. Her eyes are like saucers and it's pretty clear she's high. Faith taps me and points to a used needle on the floor by her feet. "What do we do?" I wasn't expecting to find her like this.

"We could take her back to the club," suggests Faith.

"But then Grim will know I've been here. I was hoping to have a chat, maybe convince her to get some help for his sake. I'm not sure if they've even seen each other in a while."

"You said you thought he was missing her, right? So, take her back and let him decide what to do."

"I feel like he might get mad if I do that. I've got an idea," I announce, looking around. "Let's tidy up, make this place more presentable."

Faith shrugs, also looking around. "I saw a shop just down the road. I'll pop in and get some cleaning supplies?"

I nod, smiling gratefully. "Great." This is the sort of thing ol' ladies do at the club. If there's a crisis, they get together to clean and prepare food. I can do that part, so I jump into action and begin clearing dirty dishes.

The man is still in the kitchen. He doesn't stir, so he must be pretty wasted. I pile the dishes by the sink. There's nothing to wash them with and no hot water, so I fill the kettle. When Faith returns, she hands over a bag full of supplies. "Should we move him?" she asks, nodding to the man.

I shake my head. "He seems out of it. Let's just clean up, and if she's still not with it when we've finished, we'll come back tomorrow." Faith nods in agreement.

GRIM

When I get back to the club, I head for the stairs, but Mav's voice halts my rush. "In here," he mutters.

I sigh heavily. "Do we have to do this now, Mav?"

"Pres," he reminds me. "And yes, we do."

I sit down and he fixes me with his hard stare. I smirk and remind him, "That doesn't work on me."

"Nothing seems to work on you lately, brother. What the fuck is going on?"

"I told you, I'm good."

"Bullshit. Man, we're like brothers, real brothers. The fact you ain't confiding in me is fucking painful. We're always in it together."

I roll my eyes. We've been saying that same shit for years, but lately, it doesn't feel like it. "You got Rylee and the kid now—" I begin, but I stop talking when Mav scoffs.

"Tell me this isn't because you're jealous I've settled down?"

"Of course, it's not!" I snap. "I like Rylee, she's good for you. Sometimes I even like her kid."

He smiles, knowing I hate kids. "That's huge," he admits, and I find myself grinning too. We're never mad for long. "Since we got back here, things have been crazy, and now it's settling down, you've been distant."

I shrug. "The road's calling me, brother," I confess.

Mav sits straighter. "I can't do this without you, Grim. We're changing this place together. You know your dad would have wanted it run this way, he'd be so proud of us now." My pops hated the way Eagle was running things in the last few years of his life. He didn't keep it a secret either, and often came to blows with the President back then.

"Don't do that," I mutter. "It's a shitty move."

"If you need a few days on the road, I'll get you a good run out."

"It's not that simple, and you know it isn't. It's not me, staying still . . . settling down. I wanna be on the road, just me and the lady."

"That bike isn't your lady, Grim. You need to find someone real, and then you'll see why I stay. Rylee makes it worthwhile. I get that urge too, brother. I miss our freedom, but we can't do that forever."

"Says who? Where's the rule book on life, Mav? I don't want an ol' lady or kids. I wanna pack a bag at the last minute and drive into the sunset whenever I feel like it."

"Is it the work with Arthur?" he asks.

I shake my head. "You keep saying 'work with' but lately, it's 'work for'. We're his bitches, and if we're not careful, we'll end up doing dark shit, just like your dad did."

"Eagle wasn't smart. I am. I've worked too hard for this club to go back down that path."

"Who're you trying to convince?"

"I don't have to convince anyone, I'm the fucking President. But let's not forget, I didn't make these decisions alone, Grim. I took it all to the table and the brothers voted. I'm nothing like Eagle, I consult you all on business."

I stand and head over to the cabinet where Mav keeps the rum. Unscrewing the cap on a new bottle, I pour two glasses. "I've been going to see her," I mutter.

"Who?"

"Carol."

"Your mum Carol?" He gasps, and I nod. "She's still alive?"

"Yes. I haven't been to see her fucking corpse . . . although I may as well have done."

I pass him a drink and take a seat again. "She's not good then?"

"Nah, she's a mess. She's still living in that cesspit, surrounded by dirty needles and rubbish."

"Sorry, brother."

"It is what it is." I shrug. "I guess I thought she'd have cleaned up her act after all this time. I've been every week for the last few months and it's the same story every time. She wants cash to get her next fix, she ain't interested in me."

"You wanna get her some help? We can sort that out."

I shake my head again. "What's the point? She isn't ready to get help, and it won't work until she is."

"You should have come to me, man. Don't carry shit like that on your own."

CHAPTER THREE

HADLEY

We spent hours cleaning Carol's place. When we were done, she still wasn't in a fit state to discuss Grim, so we left. Today, we're heading back to try again. This time, we're armed with clean clothes, food, and toiletries.

The front door is still ajar, so we slip inside, happy to see the place still clean and tidy. The guy from the kitchen is gone, which is a relief cos who knows what he's capable of. I begin putting food into the cupboards, and Faith uncovers the hot pie we took from the fresh batch Brea had just baked. "Who the hell are you?" I spin around and come face-to-face with Carol. She's standing on shaky legs and gripping onto the door frame for support.

"Hey, I'm Hadley, and this is Faith—"

"I told you lot before, I don't have the kid here, he lives with his dad!"

"Erm . . ." I glance at Faith, who looks just as confused as me. "We're not from child services."

She lets out a sigh of relief. "Thank fuck because I couldn't even tell you where he's taken the kid."

"What kid?" asks Faith.

"Xzavier," she snaps, frowning. "Who are you again?"

"Concerned neighbours," I cut in before Faith can answer. "We wanted to check on you because we hadn't seen you for a while, so we came over yesterday and noticed you weren't feeling well. We gave the place a little clean, I hope you don't mind." I take the hot pie from Faith and hold it out. "We got you some food."

Carol eyes it warily before taking it. "It smells good."

"It's the best." I hand her a plastic knife and fork we brought with us.

She takes a seat at the table and begins tucking into the pie. I hand her a bottle of water. "So, you live round here?" she asks through mouthfuls of food, and I nod. "I ain't seen you before and I've been here a long time."

"We just moved in . . . a few months ago. Do you have any more kids apart from Xzavier?"

"Yeah, a grown one."

"How old?" I ask, busying myself with putting the other food items away.

"Hudson is thirty-something, thirty-five maybe, and Xzavier is sixteen."

"Wow, big age gap," says Faith, smiling. "How do they feel about one another?"

"They don't know each other. You sure you're not cops?" She narrows her eyes suspiciously.

"No. Is there anything you need?" I ask.

She pushes the plate away, only half eating the pie. "I could use some cash," she mutters, looking away.

"Sorry, I'm all out. What do you need? Maybe I can get it for you next time."

"I just needed some toiletries," she lies.

"We got you covered," says Faith, pointing to the bag on the side. "There's some clothes in there too."

"Like Mary fucking Poppins," mutters Carol bitterly.

"We should go," I say, taking Faith's arm. "We'll call again soon."

Outside, Faith drags me behind a wall. "I can hear a motorbike," she hisses, and sure enough, the rumbling engine pulls onto the street, stopping outside Carol's.

"Shit, he's here?"

"Did he say he'd seen her?"

I shake my head. "It was cryptic. He didn't mean to mention her to me."

"We need to go before he sees us. Are you going to tell him he has a brother?" she asks, and I shrug. I just wanted to help, but now I feel like this is getting out of hand.

GRIM

I stare at Mum. She's up and about, and the place is spotless. I follow her into the kitchen. "Everything okay?" I ask, wiping my finger along the clean counter-top.

"Why wouldn't it be?"

"Just . . .well, I haven't seen you up and about for a long time."

"Maybe you come at the wrong time."

I open a cupboard door and frown at the tinned food stacked neatly inside. "You went shopping?"

"Yes. I do eat."

"I thought you didn't have money?"

She sighs with irritation. "I didn't, and you didn't give me any either, if I remember correctly. In fact, you never do. So, why do you care if I've been to the supermarket?"

"Of course, I care. I offer to get you food, but you never take it."

"I'm a grown woman. I can do my own shopping. Why are you here, Hudson?" I hate how she questions me like I shouldn't be here. This was once my home too.

"I'm just checking in, Mum. It's what normal families do, check on one another."

She scoffs. "Because we're so normal. If you want to help, I need money for bills."

And there it is, the quest for her next fix yet again. "Whatever. If you have bills, hand them to me and I'll go pay. I'm not giving you money to spend on drugs."

"Look at this place," she snaps. "I've changed. I'm getting help."

"You don't change in less than forty-eight hours. I gotta go," I mutter, stomping out.

As I start my bike, Mav calls my phone. "Yep?" I answer.

"You wanna do some good?"

"Does it involve Arthur Taylor?"

He laughs. "No. I'll text you the address. Meet me in ten."

∞

Mav meets me at the end of the road of the address he texted to me. I turn off my bike and remove my helmet. "See that house?" he asks, pointing to a large house on the end. "The shelter got a call from a woman they've been supporting. She was asking for help but got cut off. They think the husband came home and caught her using a phone she'd hidden from him. The police can't get anyone out to do a welfare check for another hour at least. I thought you'd wanna do something good, get back to what we came here for." I nod. Doing shit like this helps me feel better.

We step off our bikes, leaving them at the end of the road in case of nosy neighbours. As we step closer, I notice the house is quiet. There's no screaming or shouting, but as we approach the door, there's the faint sound of a baby crying. We can't take a baby on our bikes, so Mav sends off a text to the prospect back at the clubhouse, telling him we'll need more appropriate transport.

I knock on the door and then ring the doorbell. We wait a second before it's ripped open and an angry-looking man in a suit glares at us. "What?" he barks. I run my eyes over him, taking in his shortness of breath and the way his chest heaves with the exertion. His fists are curled tightly, and his hair is stuck to his forehead where sweat beads linger.

"We were in the area—" Mav begins.

"Not today," the man hisses, pushing the door to close it.

I stick my boot in at the last minute and the door bounces back. "Actually, today, right this second, is perfect," I say, adding a smile.

"Can't you hear my child crying. I need to attend to her."

"Can't your wife do that?" asks Mav.

"She isn't here," he hisses.

"Oh . . . see, that makes no sense because we were told she was," I say, suddenly shoving the door hard and gaining entry. It takes him by surprise and he has no time to react as I step into the large hallway. My boots crunch on the broken glass of a vase which lays in pieces, its contents spread across the wooden floor. "Is she this way?" I ask, pointing to the living room.

"I don't know who the hell you are, but I'm calling the police," he yells angrily, stepping in front of me and blocking my path.

"Do that," suggests Mav.

"They're already on their way, so it might hurry them along," I add.

He visibly swallows, and for the first time since we arrived, he looks worried. "Why are the police coming?"

"First, because they wanted to help your wife, who I think might be in that room," I say, pointing again to the living room. "But now, they might have to arrest me because if I find what I think I'm going to, I'll hurt you."

"It's not what it looks like," he begins as I push him out of my way. Mav stays with him, and I enter the room and spot his wife lying face-down on the carpet. The room is a mess and there's droplets of blood dotted around the cream rug.

"Don't tell me," I drawl, "she fell."

"She's cheating on me!" he shouts.

I turn, connecting my fist with his jaw. The crack is deafening in the silence. He groans, gripping his face. "I don't care if she fucked another man right in front of you. Don't lay your hands on a woman!"

He nods, unable to speak because I suspect his jaw is broken. "I'll take care of her," says Mav, letting me take free rein on this dick. When I've landed my last kick, he's a heap on the floor, just like his wife. "Go get the kid," orders Mav, holding the man's unconscious wife in his arms. "We need to get her to the doc."

"I'll take her, you get the kid."

"Grim, now is not the time to give me the 'I hate kids' speech. Just get the damn baby so we can leave."

I huff, stomping upstairs and following the sound of crying until I find the red-faced little thing all tense and angry in its cot. I scoop it up, and it immediately stops the noise. "Thank the lord," I whisper to no one in particular. "Let's get something straight," I mutter, spotting a pink change bag in the corner. "I don't like babies, not even pretty ones like you," I pick up the bag and continue, "but I'll make this exception because you deserve better. And so does your mum. But if you scream like that again while in my arms, I'm likely to freak out, so let's just be nice to one another and make the best of this terrible situation."

Outside, Mav has put the woman into a car. Ghost nods in greeting from the driver's seat. "Put her in the chair," he tells me, pointing to the safety chair in the back.

I lay the baby in it and stare at the straps with confusion. "How do you know it's a girl?" I ask.

Ghost frowns. "She's dressed in pink."

I shrug. "Makes sense." Mav shoves me out the way and expertly straps the baby into the chair. "We'll meet you at the club," he tells Ghost.

※

The doc's been in with the woman for an hour. Ghost is now holding the kid with that dopey look on his face, the one everyone gets when there's a baby around. Suddenly, the main door opens, and Arthur Taylor stomps in, flanked by two of his brothers. "Gentlemen," he says, coldly. "We need to talk."

I follow Mav and Arthur into the office. The two Taylor brothers remain at the back of Arthur's chair, and I snigger. I hate the whole dangerous vibe they try to give off. If he was so dangerous, he wouldn't need Tweedle-Dum and Tweedle-Dee by his side.

"What can we do for you?" asks Mav calmly.

"Have you just been on Lennon Street?" he snaps, and Mav nods. "At number twenty?" Mav nods again. "You just beat the fuck out of Nick Cambridge!" he yells.

"If you mean the shit bag who hurt his wife, then yeah, it was me," I admit.

Arthur glares at me. "If you weren't the fucking VP, I'd slit your throat right now."

I arch a brow. "Try it."

"Don't fucking push me," he screams.

Mav raises his hand, a sign for us to keep it peaceful. "Who is he?"

Arthur takes a calming breath. "He's the CEO of Cambridge Enterprises, a multi-millionaire with a chain of high-class casinos and a man I have just associated myself with. He's put a fucking hit out on the men who took his wife and child."

I exchange a look with Mav. "You know what we do, Arthur. He was beating his wife. She's a mess."

"I don't care if she's fucking dead right now. I have to get her back to him."

"Not a chance," I say, laughing angrily. "I don't care who the fuck he is."

"The police know. The women's centre called them," adds Mav. "This can't be brushed under the carpet."

"He can sort that out, but I have to get her back. He wants you dead. He offered me a lot of money to find and kill you." He looks at me.

"Then do it," I snap, "because that's the only way she's getting out of here."

"Why the fuck would you go into his home wearing your kuttes?" asks Arthur.

"Cos we wanted him to know who the fuck he was messing with," I state.

"Clearly, you didn't know who you were messing with."

"You'll have to stall him," says Mav.

"I can't do that. It's not how it works. Besides, he might have others out looking for you."

"And you want the money first?" I mutter.

"Would you still be breathing if that was the case?" he hisses. "Fuck, Mav, we need a plan and we need it now."

HADLEY

I follow Meli into the room where our newest arrival is lying on the bed. She's so badly beat, even Meli winces. "Hey, I'm Meli, and this is Hadley."

"Hey," she almost whispers.

"Do you need anything?" I ask.

She shakes her head. I peer into the Moses basket and smile down at the tiny baby sleeping soundly beside her mum. "She's gorgeous. How old is she?"

"Two weeks."

"She's gonna be a heart-breaker, that's for sure. She even had the guys melting over her."

"Where am I?"

"You're at the clubhouse of The Perished Riders MC. Our brother is the President here. You called the women's shelter, but they couldn't get the police out fast enough, so they sent us instead," Meli explains.

"You're safe now," I add.

"I'm never safe," she mutters.

"We help women just like you all the time. I'm a lawyer, and I can help you with a restraining order or whatever else you need."

She half smiles, but it doesn't quite reach her bruised eyes. "That will never happen. He'll find me and take me home."

"Not if you don't want to go," says Meli. "We won't let him."

"You don't know my husband. How will you stop him?"

Ghost steps into the room, holding up a baby's bottle. "I fed her when she arrived, but she's due again, according to Gracie. And I'll stop him. Trust me."

I exchange a smirk with Meli. We've seen this before, when his brother, Scar, brought Gracie back to the club. "Well, we'll leave you in Ghost's capable hands," Meli sniggers, hooking her arm through mine and pulling me from the room.

∞

I close my eyes and lean my head back against the large oak tree. I left Meli inside cooking up a plan with Rosey to help keep the new woman here. They both live in a dream world. Rosey is so far off reality, I think she should be sectioned.

I hear his footsteps as he approaches, sensing it's Grim, then he drops down beside me. I keep my eyes closed, letting my senses take in his manly smell of oil and leather mixed with a little hint of woodsy aftershave. The good news is I don't smell alcohol, and when I finally open my eyes, he's staring right at me. He looks happy, like a weight has been lifted. "Everything okay?" I ask.

"Better than okay."

"That's good to know. Any particular reason?"

"Someone I've been worrying about is actually starting to make progress."

I try to look surprised. "That's great. Are you going to tell me who?"

"My mum."

I didn't expect him to be so open, and it takes me a second to react. "Shit," I mutter. "I can't believe you've been to see her."

"Yeah, I know Dad would probably think it was a waste of time, but yah know, she's still my ma."

I nod. "True. How is she?"

He takes a breath and smiles, tipping his head back and staring at the dusky sky. "She's doing better than I've seen in a long time."

Silence stretches out, and I pluck up the courage to probe some more. "While you've been away from her, what do you think she's been doing?"

He scoffs. "You mean apart from getting wasted every day?" He shrugs. "Who knows?"

"Maybe she met someone, maybe she had kids?"

He laughs. "You're kidding, right? If you saw her these days, you'd realise how crazy that sounds. She's a mess and has been for a long time. No, she's been too busy taking drugs for anything like that."

CHAPTER FOUR

GRIM

"Please," I watch my mum fall to her knees, grabbing onto the leg of her latest love, "I can change. Don't leave me." Even at the tender age of thirteen, I know she's kidding herself. She'll never change, she'll never stop taking the drugs or drinking. She couldn't do it for me and Dad, and when she tells us she will, it lasts no more than a few days. That's how I've ended up here, watching her beg another man to stay.

He looks to me for help, and I just shrug. I can't wade in there. She'll get violent, and I'm about to meet Jenifer Wood. I think she's finally going to show me what she shows all the boys at school, and I can't turn up with scratches and bruises. When he sees I'm not going to help, he kicks her. It's hard enough to make her cough, and she releases him. I wince. Fucking moron. He didn't need to hurt her. "Dick," I mutter, reaching a hand down to Mum to help her up.

"What did you say to me?" he growls.

"I said you're a dick! Get the fuck out."

"You little shit, you don't know who you're messing with!"

Mum turns her begging to me. "Please, Hudson, don't upset him or he'll leave."

"He's leaving anyway, Ma. Get off the floor."

"Do you blame me with the shit I've had to put up with for the last six months?" he yells.

I roll my eyes. "Yeah, Mike, I feel real sorry for you."

"Mark! My fucking name is Mark, and you know it!" he yells, and I snigger. It always gets him.

"Hudson Scott," my mum hisses, "apologise right now."

I shake my head. "No, Ma. He just kicked you. I ain't apologising."

"Your kid is fucking unruly!" Mark continues his barrage of reasons he's leaving when in actual fact, we both know he'll go get drunk, fuck some whore, and return here tomorrow begging my mum to forgive him. And she will!

My phone rings. "Dad," I say, relieved to hear a friendly voice. "Can you come get me? She's drunk."

"Jesus, that stupid bitch," Dad hisses. He gives her chance after chance, but she can't ever stay sober. He got full custody of me when I was six years old, but the weekends are supposed to be when she has me.

After I hang up, Mark begins yelling some more and throwing shit around. I hunch over to protect Mum and it pisses him off, so he comes for me. He's been dying to for weeks. He grips my leather jacket. I'm too young to wear the club's kutte just yet, but wearing the jacket makes me feel part of the club. He pulls me to stand straight. "Fucking biker trash. What kind of dad lets his son run with a gang?"

I stare him in the eyes. "It ain't no gang, Mikey."

"And this is where you tell me it's a brotherhood, right?"

"It's where I don't bother to explain cos I can't educate stupid."

"You little—"

My knife goes in so cleanly, I have to look down to check I got him. His eyes tell me I did, but I didn't feel the usual resistance. Blood drips from my fingers and I smile, satisfied I got him. "Now, get your hands off me or this knife's gonna go all the way through."

He releases me, and I grin just before I withdraw the blade. Mum begins to scream. I grab her, covering her mouth and talking calmly into her ear, asking her to not panic and keep quiet. She eventually nods, and I uncover her mouth. She stares wide-eyed at the bloodied weapon hanging by my side. "You're just like your father," she whispers.

I wake with a start. I'm cold and realise I'm still outside but it's now dark. "Good nap?" asks Hadley, looking amused.

"How long was I out?" I stretch, groaning at the pain in my back.

"Twenty minutes tops. I was just about to wake you. It's getting cold out here."

She shivers, and I place an arm around her shoulder and tug her towards me. "Sorry, it's not like me to sleep like that."

"You must have needed it."

I stare up at the twinkling stars just beginning to make an appearance. It's been years since I've thought about my childhood, let alone that part. I shudder. "I need a drink."

"Or," says Hadley, pushing up to stand, "we could do something else."

"Like?"

She bites on her lower lip, and my eyes are drawn to it. I frown, then shudder again. My head must be fucked if I'm noticing things Hadley does. "I know a really nice coffee place. We could head there for an hour."

"Why would I want to go to a coffee place when I have a bar right in there with my brothers?" She looks down at the ground in disappointment, and I feel like a dick. "Actually, maybe a coffee would be good. I bet Arthur's still in there anyway."

∞

We go on the bike. I've never had Hadley on the back of mine, not since she was a kid. It feels different now she's older, but I can't explain why, so I try not to think about it. She directs me, and I stop outside a cosy-looking place with twinkling lights in the window and a warm glow about it. Inside, customers are talking in low voices, and there's a woman in the corner singing a soulful tune. It's relaxing, but I've never been in a place like it, and as we take a seat by the window and Hadley shrugs out of her jacket, I feel uncomfortable, like everyone is staring at me.

The waitress heads over. "Two Colombian roast, please," Hadley orders.

"You got a thing about Colombia," I mutter.

"Why are you so tense?" she asks, grinning.

"It's not really my sort of place, is it, Hads? Coffee, small lights, singers."

"I bet you've never even been to a place like this," she says, looking around. "How can you not love it? When it's really cold, they have an open fire burning. It's such an amazing little place."

"Do you come here a lot?"

She nods, genuinely looking happy. "All the time. It's my quiet place where I can avoid the club drama or hide from Meli."

I grin. "You hide from your own twin? Don't you have the thing that connects you so she can sense where you are?"

She laughs again. "Sometimes. Since all the stuff with Ripper, I doubt the connection. If we had that, I would have known."

The mood shifts, and I sigh. "How could you? I think we've both punished ourselves

enough over that. When Mav and I came back, he told me to watch her, and I didn't see it. I mean, I sensed she didn't like him, but it's Meli, she doesn't like many people."

"I guess it's in the past. Mama said we shouldn't keep going over it. Speaking of which, have you told Mav about your mum?"

I nod before changing the subject. The dream earlier fucked my head up and I don't feel like talking about her now. "It feels weird being out the club with you like this. I don't think we've ever done it."

She chews on her lip, then says, "When we were younger, we used to sit under the tree." I frown cos I don't remember. She smiles, shrugging it off. "It was a long time ago."

"When we were kids, you annoyed me," I confess, remembering how she'd watch me all the time. Her little nose would poke out over the top of the damn books she always had her head in. The brothers used to give me grief for it, and I'd take it out on her, purposely being mean. "I was a prick back then."

She shrugs. "Again, it was a long time ago. We've both grown up."

"Hadley, why haven't you settled down or at least dated?" I never see her slipping out dressed up for a date, unlike her sister.

The coffees arrive and she stares down at hers for a moment. "I just haven't met the one who makes me stop and notice."

I watch her take a careful sip of the hot liquid. "Why are you waiting? Meli's always on dates, trying to find the one, and you're just holding back . . . but for what? A guy ain't gonna fall from the sky and land at your feet."

"You wouldn't understand," she mutters.

"Try me. I'm not being a dick—I really do want to know."

Hadley sighs. "I want to wait until I find someone special. Meli doesn't care about anyone. She likes sex and it doesn't matter who with." That answer hurts, but I hide my reaction by drinking some coffee. "I'm not a prude or anything, I just want a nice guy."

"But how will you meet him if you're always at the club or working?"

She looks around. "In places like this. The type of guy I want isn't going to be in a nightclub. I won't make the same mistake as Mum." And suddenly, it makes sense. She's avoiding men like Eagle.

HADLEY

I shift uncomfortably under his intense stare. "Do you think you'll meet a man in the MC?" he asks.

I want to tell him so badly how I feel, but he doesn't feel the same, and I won't embarrass myself by confessing all just because we're sharing one small, brief moment. "I don't know. Maybe if someone new comes to the club."

"What about Meli?" he asks, and that's the real answer he wants to know because I've sat back and observed him watching her for years. Not that Meli cares. She's not interested in Grim, and she'd rather chop off her own head than be with him, but it still hurts me, knowing how badly he wants her and not me.

"Who knows? Meli changes her mind like the weather. She's got an eye on the Taylor men right now."

Grim screws up his face in disgust. "Mafia?"

"This week. Next week, it could be a cop for all I know. Like I said, she's too indecisive."

We finish our coffees, and I marvel at the fact I got Grim into my happy space at least once. I pay the bill, much to his annoyance, and we head back out to his bike. My favourite part of the whole night has been holding onto him like he belongs to me. "I'll drop you home," he says, throwing his leg over the bike.

"Aren't you staying?"

"I'm gonna find a place I like. My sort of place."

"Take me," I say a little too eagerly, and he grins. "Please? I'd like to see where you hang out. It's only fair seeing as I dragged you here."

He ponders the thought, then nods. "Fine. But you'll hate it."

He's right . . . I hate it. It's a small bar and it's dark inside—dark wood, dark carpets, and dirty windows. The lights are dim, and I think it's probably from dirt. There are a few older men scattered around, each with a half-drunk pint in front of them.

Grim shakes hands with the barman in greeting, so he must come here regularly. "Two pints, please," he orders, and I gasp.

"Pints!"

"I had coffee, now you have to try what I like."

"Can't we at least have a whiskey?"

He smirks and changes the order, then we take our drinks and sit down. "What do you think?" he asks.

I look around, trying to find positives, but there's nothing, so I grimace. "It's different."

He laughs. "You hate it."

"I don't hate it. I don't love it either."

"Nobody talks. I think it's where some of these guys come to die," he whispers, and I laugh. "Occasionally, Alf over there, his wife marches in and drags him home. That's the most excitement this place sees."

"So, why do you like it so much?"

Grim shrugs. "Nobody cares. It doesn't matter who I am because they don't even look up. I can sit here in silence and no one bothers me. I don't know them, and they don't know me."

"You like the anonymity?"

A woman comes in carrying an armful of roses. She makes a beeline for us, and Grim shakes his head as she mutters about buying a rose for his love. "You buy the pretty lady flower?" she says in broken English, and I giggle.

"She's not my lady."

"But you like her to be, no?"

He glares at me for help, but I just smile back, enjoying his discomfort. "Jesus," he mutters, reaching into his pocket. The woman smiles at me like she's won. "I'll take one if it means you'll go." He slams a note on the table, and the woman inspects it before offering me a rose and I take it.

"She a good woman. You have two babies. You marry her."

"I don't think so," he scoffs.

The woman places her hand on mine and closes her eyes. "Yes," she eventually says. "You marry. Two babies." She opens her eyes suddenly and stares hard at me. "But be careful, it's a bumpy road," she whispers before leaving. I stare after her, bewildered by her strange comment.

"What did she say?" he asks.

"That I should be careful."

We both laugh uncomfortably, then his smile fades. "She's right, though."

CHAPTER FIVE

GRIM

The flower seller leaves awkward feelings hanging between us. The ease of the night so far, is long gone, I'm left wondering if Hadley sees this as something more than a pleasant evening. Because it's been nice, and it took my mind off Mum, but the last thing I want is to start something up with Hadley. She's not my type, and while she might intrigue me, there's nothing romantic in it. Besides, I've slept with her twin, so this can never amount to anything. I decide to clear the air and take a deep breath.

"Just so we're on the same page . . . this," I move my hand between us, "is nothing more than a . . ." I trail off, lost for what the word is to make it sound nothing like a date.

Her cheeks redden. "It's nothing," she says very clearly and leaves me with no doubt that we're on the same page.

"Great. I'm pleased we understand each other . . . it just felt weird with her—"

"Please, let's not make it worse. I already told you, I'm not looking for a guy like you." She almost scoffs and rolls her eyes. It's a little uncalled for, but I force a smile anyway. "Maybe we should head back," she adds, knocking her drink down in one. "Or if you wanna stay and, yah know, meet someone, I can make my own way."

I laugh, picking up my own drink and doing the same. "Hadley, I'm not that much of a dick I'd let you go home alone."

When I wake the next day, it's almost ten o'clock. I never sleep in, so it surprises me. Heading down to the kitchen after my shower, I find everyone out apart from Brea, who's mixing something. "There're leftovers in the fridge," she tells me, hardly bothering to look up from her batter.

I take the coffee pot and pour myself a cup. "Mama B, when was the last time you saw my ma?" I ask, taking a seat and scooping my finger through the mixture she's beating. I pop it in my mouth and hum in approval. She narrows her eyes and swipes at me playfully.

"You used to do that as a kid. I let you because you were too thin when we first got you here and you needed to fatten up. Now you're an adult, it's not okay," she jokes.

"I went to see her."

Brea stops mixing and wipes her hands down her apron, keeping her eyes fixed on me. "How is she?"

"Up and down. Things seem to be up at the moment, but I'm not holding my breath."

"I don't remember the last time I saw her, Grim. But I can tell you I've never seen her looking well."

"Did she come around looking for me when I was a kid? Yah know, after Dad took me from her?" She bites her lip, and I know she's holding back. "B, I'm an adult now, I should know the truth, and Dad isn't around to ask."

Brea takes a seat. "She did come here a few times, and once, she even got a hold of you and tried to walk out, but your dad wouldn't let her. When it came down to it, it was money she wanted and she'd threaten to take you if he didn't hand it over. That stopped once your dad died. She knew she'd never get a penny from Eagle or the brothers." I nod. I knew it deep down, but hearing the words out loud brings a lump to my throat. I swallow it down. "It's an illness, Grim, just like the drink. She got herself hooked on that stuff when she was too young to understand the implications. And she didn't know how to take care of a baby. No one showed her, and she tried, but it wasn't good enough. We gave you a good childhood, made sure you were loved and happy, and you weren't missing a female figure in your life."

"I know," I say. "Just something inside doesn't let me stop checking in on her. I hate doing it, but I can't just walk away like she's nothing, which is fucked up seeing as it's exactly what she did to me."

Brea places her hand over mine. "I don't think it was an easy choice. If anything, it made her worse because, suddenly, she had nothing to stop her. Nothing to fight for. She knew she'd never get you back from this club. We look after our own. And we tried to help her, I promise we did, but she was too far gone."

"If Dad was still around, do you think he'd check in on her?"

Brea smiles. "He had a soft spot for her, that's for sure. He'd tell you not to bother with her, but I think he'd secretly be checking she was okay, just like you are."

I lean over the table and kiss her on the cheek. "Thanks, Mama B."

"You know what he'd also say?" she asks, and I shake my head. "He'd ask why the hell you haven't settled down and given him a grandbaby yet."

I laugh, heading for the exit before we get too deep. "I ain't making the same mistake he did, and I've got too much lovin' for one woman."

I step out for air and spot Hadley under the oak tree. As I head over, I realise it's becoming a regular thing. "Maybe you wanna marry the tree?" I ask, smirking.

She looks up from her book. "I have a day off and thought I'd spend it wisely."

"Normal women shop or meet friends for lunch."

"Actually, I wanted to shop, but Mav won't let me out without an escort. He said something is going on with the club and we can't go out alone."

"Right." I dig my boot in the dirt. "Two things. One, you never go shopping, so what the hell is wrong? And two, why don't you just take a brother?"

She laughs. "I wanted to change up my wardrobe. I'm tired of wearing baggy stuff." I arch a brow at her confession. Hadley always wears clothes that cover her up, the bigger the better. "You said it yourself that a guy isn't just gonna fall from the sky. So, I'm making changes, and I didn't want to make one of the guys endure a shopping trip with me. I have no clue what I'm doing, and Meli's busy."

"I'll take you," I offer before I even think about it.

She smiles wide. "Really?"

I shrug. "I don't have much else to do at the moment. Go tell Mav you're heading out, and I'll get my bike keys."

HADLEY

The store is huge. I feel overwhelmed as we head inside and instantly doubt my decision, but I square my shoulders and internally berate myself for being so negative. I can do this. Meli always does this, so it can't be that bad. I spent the entire night thinking about how to get Grim to notice me, like really notice me like he does my twin. I've spent so long in the shadows because of the way my dad treated us that I've been too scared to flourish for fear of embarrassing myself.

"Where do I start?" I ask.

Grim looks around, then at me with a blank expression. "Why are you asking me?"

Panic sets in again and I turn back towards the exit. "You're right, what the hell am I doing here? And with you?"

He rushes to block my path, preventing me from leaving. "Okay, let's just calm down and take a breath." He looks around again. "It can't be that hard to find some clothes, right? I've seen women do it before, and it doesn't look that hard." We're both out of our depth, and I begin to laugh. "What's so funny?" he asks.

"Look at us getting into a panic over some clothes."

He grins before grabbing my hand. "Come on, let's find you something that doesn't resemble a bin bag."

I revel in the feel of his rough hand gripping my own. Just that simple touch makes me feel alive, like I'm shining beside him and everyone is envious because I'm touching him and they aren't. Women stare our way as we pass, and I know they're not looking at me. He stops suddenly. "Here," he mutters, grabbing some jeans and holding them up. "What size are you?"

I point to the hanger with my correct size, and he swaps for them. I've never worn skinny jeans, always preferring the baggier ones. Next, he points to some T-shirts. They're the kind Meli likes with slogans across the front. I shake my head and reluctantly let go of his hand so I can find something for myself. Something that won't remind him of my twin.

"Can I help?" asks a store assistant.

"I need clothes. I'm looking to change my entire wardrobe and I have no idea where to start." Her eyes light up like I'm her dream come true, and she beckons me to follow her as she marches through the rails of clothes, grabbing items as she passes. She then points me in the direction of the changing room. Grim looks on with a smile playing on his lips as she shoves me forward and then follows me.

"I'll wait right out here and hand you outfits to try," she says when I step into a small cubicle. She pulls a curtain across, and I release a breath.

I try numerous pairs of jeans with different shirts, fitted jumpers, and then she begins passing dresses my way. I show her each outfit, and if she likes it, she then forces me to go and show Grim. By the time I'm finished, I'm exhausted.

I make my way to the checkout, and she hands me bags already filled with my new clothes. I hold out my credit card, but she shakes her head. "No, ma'am, your husband already paid."

"Oh, he's—"

"Thanks," says Grim, taking the bags from her. "Let's go, my little swan."

I follow him from the shop, confused. "How much do I owe you?"

"Nothing. Mav took care of it."

"Mav?"

"Yeah, he sent me a text saying to treat you on his card, so I did."

I'm suspicious. Maverick never treats me, especially not to that amount of money. I'll have to square it with him later.

GRIM

"Where the fuck have you been?" Mav demands when I step into church half an hour late. The guys all stare at me, waiting patiently for my answer.

I drop down in my usual spot and shrug. "I'm here now, aren't I?"

Mav huffs but decides to continue with the meeting. "As I was saying, Nick Cambridge is recovering in hospital after Grim's brutal beating." He glances at me with a smirk. "But my dilemma is, Arthur is currently using this prick. He's planning a big job on the casino—"

I sit up straighter. "He's robbing the place?"

"Something like that. He's pulling off simultaneous jobs, hitting two or three of his casinos in one go. I don't know the details, I just know Arthur's in a really difficult position." "Poor Arthur," I mutter sarcastically.

"He thinks we should return Harriett to him."

The men become unsettled, grumbling and complaining. "What does that make us if we send her back to a monster?" asks Ghost. "He could kill her, and that will be on us."

"I'm with you," says Mav. "I've told Arthur my answer is no. But that means we have to put the club on lockdown."

I immediately think of Mum and not being able to check on her. "Do we need to be so extreme?" I ask. "We just need to be alert and ready for anything."

"Maybe," mutters Mav.

"Arthur's our inside man. If Cambridge is gonna attack, he'll know about it and warn us. We just gotta be smart," I add.

"And get Hadley on the case. She can get us a court order," suggests Gears. "The sooner we get Harriett covered, the better."

"Okay, let's go with it for now, but any sign of an attack and we're locking down. I won't risk the club."

Mav bangs the gavel on the table, and the brothers begin to disperse. I get up, but Mav shakes his head, nodding for me to sit back down, which I do. Once the room is clear, he fixes me with his eyes. "So?"

"So?" I repeat.

"You've been gone for hours, and you didn't answer your mobile. Last night was the same."

"You told Hadley she had to take someone with her today, so she took me."

He frowns, taking a minute to absorb that information. "You took Hadley shopping?" I nod. "Why?"

"She needed to go. Oh, and if she asks, you paid."

He frowns deeper. "I paid? She'd never believe that."

"She would if you agree. Brother, she needed a new wardrobe and—"

"Hold on one goddamn minute," he interrupts, standing. "Let me get this straight. You took Hadley shopping for clothes and then you paid?"

I shrug. "It's not a big deal."

"Are you joking right now? This is you . . . and Hadley . . . you can't stand her!"

"She's not so bad now she's older."

Mav's eyes widen and he stares open-mouthed. "Oh, Jesus, you like Hadley."

I groan, standing. "I do not. Grow the fuck up."

"You like her! You like Hadley!"

"Stop saying that. You've lost your mind. Maybe she's the only one who's fucking noticed I'm struggling, Mav. Maybe Hadley checks in to make sure I'm doing okay."

He looks taken aback. "Am I missing something? Aren't you okay?"

I shake my head slowly, staring hard at the ground. "No, I'm not."

"I know you're struggling with staying in one place," he says.

I head for the door. "That's not it," I snap. "It's just part of the bigger problem."

I stomp out of church and take the stairs two at a time. Almost crashing into Hadley as I round the corner, she slams back against the wall. We stare at each other for a few moments, her panting in shock and me in anger. My eyes run over her lips, and for the briefest second, I wonder what they taste like. The spell is broken when

I hear Mav calling my name. Hadley must sense my anguish because she opens her bedroom door and yanks me inside, slamming it closed and locking it. Then, she smiles. "You okay?"

"Not really, Hads," I mutter.

She sits on her bed and looks up at me. "You need to talk about it?"

I wander over to the window and stare at the field stretching out for miles. "What's the point?"

"Talking helps. Sharing a problem and all that."

I shake my head. Truth is, I don't have a clue what the actual problem is. "I'm just having a down day. Thanks for letting me hide in here, though. Your brother is on my back lately."

I turn to face her as she slides back onto her bed and leans against the headboard. "You hate being back here," she states, but I don't reply. Part of me does, cos it brings back memories, good and bad, but lately, mainly bad. "You want to hit the road."

"That's what bikers do, right?" I ask, forcing a smile. "The road is where I'm happiest."

"But now Mav's settled here as the Pres, it's not so easy to up and leave?"

"I could just go without him." But I know I won't. He's like a blood brother. "He's happy here with Rylee, and I'm happy for him, but it's not me. It's not my life."

Hadley takes a deep breath. "I could use a hand right now if you're free." She pulls a heavy-looking box from the floor to her bed. "These are old files I had couriered over from Harriett's former solicitor. She filed for divorce once but later retracted it. Apparently, they make an interesting read."

I flop down on the bed opposite her as she removes the lid. "What are you looking for exactly?" I ask, peering into the dusty box full of papers and files.

"Anything we can use to get this restraining order granted. I have a meeting with the judge bright and early."

Hadley passes me the first paper file and a highlighting pen. I smile gratefully because this is exactly what I need to take my mind off Mum and the unhappiness I have in my heart. And somehow, Hadley knows that.

CHAPTER SIX

HADLEY

I'm vaguely aware I'm uncomfortable, so I stretch out an aching arm and groan. Opening one eye, I notice sunlight streaming through the blinds and it suddenly dawns on me it's daylight. I sit up in alarm. Grim is asleep at the end of my bed with a highlighter pen still in his grasp, and we're surrounded by paperwork. "Shit!" I hiss, grabbing my phone. I have to meet the judge in less than half an hour. "Fuck . . . shit . . . damn it! Grim, wake up." I shake him, and he sits up quickly, almost headbutting me. "We fell asleep."

He looks around confused. "What day is it?"

"The day I have to meet the judge!" I rush to the bathroom, slipping out of my joggers and tee and diving under the cold spray of the shower. I hiss, waiting impatiently for it to warm up before I carelessly rub soap over my skin. Once I'm done, I squirt toothpaste onto my brush and stuff it in my mouth while wrapping myself in a towel and running back into my bedroom. Grim watches in amusement as I pull clothes from the shopping bags we filled yesterday. I find the black dress I picked out. It's perfect and something I'd usually avoid, but today, I don't have time to talk myself out of it as I run back to the bathroom, grabbing underwear as I go.

I'm staring at myself in the bathroom mirror with a mascara wand in my hand when the door opens and Grim steps in. He raises his eyebrows, letting his eyes run down my body. "Wow."

"Please don't say anything because I don't have time to change and—"

He grips the tops of my arms and turns me to look at him. "I was going to say, you look amazing, Hads. Like, really great."

I blush. "Really?"

"Really. Now, where are you meeting this judge? I'll take you." He then picks up my toothpaste, puts some on his finger, and rubs it around his mouth.

The outfit isn't ideal for the bike, but as Grim pulls to a stop outside the courthouse and I carefully slide off, I notice how he positions his arm to help cover my modesty. I smile to myself as he hands over my bag and case file. "What will you tell the judge about me?" he asks, following me up the steps. Mav insists one of the men shadow me at work.

"That the firm hired security because of who Nick Cambridge is," she explains.

GRIM

I shudder as we step into the large, intimidating building. It's not the first time I've been inside this place, and chances are, it won't be the last. We place our belongings on the trays the security team holds out, and then we step through their body scanner before being cleared to go through. We head up some winding stone steps and stop outside a door. "Please stay quiet in there, Grim. It's really important." I nod. Hadley knocks, and a young woman opens the door and smiles wide.

"The judge is waiting for you," she says, stepping to the side so we can enter. I stay positioned by the door, and Hadley breezes into the room towards a gentleman sitting at the head of a large oak table. He stands and looks pleased to see Hadley, embracing her and kissing her on the cheek. I frown. I didn't know she was so familiar with judges and such like.

"Hadley, it's so great to see you," he gushes, pulling out the chair to his left and waiting for her to sit down.

"Thank you so much for agreeing to meet with me on such short notice."

"It's a pleasure. I'll always make time for you. How's life?" he asks, taking his seat again and staring at her like she's the most interesting person in the entire world. The young woman smiles at me as she exits the room. If I wasn't here, Hadley would be alone with this man, and that pisses me off.

I tune back into their conversation as the judge flicks his eyes to me and asks her, "Who's the oaf?"

"He's here to watch over me. The guy we're dealing with isn't above trying to stop this going through," says Hadley, placing her file on the table and turning it towards him. "Harry, you would not believe the things I've read in the last twelve hours."

I listen while Hadley goes into work mode. She's fucking awesome at it. The way she knows this case and recalls facts and dates astounds me, and even though I read those notes with her, I don't remember half of what she does. By the time she's finished pleading Harriett Cambridge's case, the judge is already buzzing his secretary to draw up the court papers.

HADLEY
Harry is putty in my hands. I smile as he signs the prevention order and hands it to me. "Amazing. I'll have this served on Mr. Cambridge today."

"Now that's out the way, will you have some breakfast with me?"

I smile politely, not wanting to offend him in case I need to work my magic on him another time. "That would be amazing, but I have so much to do. Could we arrange another time?" I ask, tucking the paperwork into my file and standing.

Harry tips his head to one side. "One day, Hadley, you'll agree to one date, and then I'll talk you into a second and a third."

I laugh, lightly touching his arm. "Harry, you know I can't wait to join you for dinner sometime, but our schedules are always clashing. Have your secretary call me to set something up." I kiss him on each cheek and head for the exit. The dress gives me a power vibe, and I march past Grim, winking at him and leading the way out.

We get outside, and I let out a relieved breath. "Harry, you know I can't wait to join you," says Grim in a screechy tone. I arch a brow at his attempt to mock me.

"I'm a little fish in a big pond, Grim. I have to play the part."

"Of a hooker?"

I gasp. "As a working woman in a man's world."

"You flirted your arse off in there. You practically pushed your tits in his face at one point."

I feel my cheeks colour, and suddenly, Dad's sneering face fills my vision. I look down at the dress and horror takes over me. Who the hell do I think I am dressing like this? I rush down the stone steps, taking off towards the tube with Grim shouting my name.

He must give up because I make the tube without him tailing me. Pushing my way through the crowded carriage, I eventually find a seat between an elderly man and a woman dressed similar to me. She doesn't look uncomfortable or out of place like I do. She fits the business woman image. I glance down at my dress again and frown. Nobody is looking at me like I'm different, and they're not laughing at me. In fact, nobody is paying me the slightest bit of attention.

I lean my head against the window and spend the ten-minute journey remembering the way my father spoke to me whenever I tried to change the way I looked.

I find myself heading straight for the oak tree when I get back to the club. My feet hurt from the low heels I'd worn to match the dress. I usually wear flats. I kick the shoes off and lower to the ground, staring out across the field.

I spot Mum heading over to me holding a mug. She smiles, hands me a coffee, and lowers to sit beside me. "You're spending a lot of time out here lately. Everything okay?" I nod. "Didn't the judge grant the restraining order?" I nod again. "Then why the long face?"

She always used to ask that question when we were little, and it brings back fond memories. "Mum, do I look like a whore?"

She almost laughs before realising I'm serious. Concern replaces her smile. "No, Hadley. Why would you ask that?"

I pluck at the dress. "It's not me, is it?"

"Why?"

"Because I never wear this kind of stuff. It's just not me."

"What is you?"

I shrug. "Baggy jumpers. Joggers."

"Clothes that cover your beautiful body," says Mum, tucking a stray hair behind my ear. "Hadley, you're beautiful, and I didn't tell you often enough when you were little because your dad . . . well, you know what he was like. You don't have to hide away."

"Why did he make me feel like the ugliest person in the world?" I whisper, and she smiles sadly.

"Because he was scared at how perfect you were, and he didn't want any man to take you away. You were his precious butterfly. He used to say you were too good for the club and he'd never let a brother marry you. He wanted you to fly away and find something or someone better."

"He didn't treat Meli like that," I point out.

"Meli didn't have it easy either. He got to her in different ways, but you know her, she's never been one to be told what to do. She drove him nuts because she was so unruly." Her smile fades, and the thought of Ripper must enter both our heads because we fall silent.

Eventually, she takes my hand. "I never told you this before, but after what I did, betraying your dad, he became bitter. He said you looked like me, too beautiful and too alluring. He was worried the brothers might look at you wrong." A tear runs down her cheek. "He became so obsessed with hiding you, he forgot about Meli. In the end, she got hurt instead."

I wrap my arms around her. "Sorry, Mum, I didn't mean to remind you of all the bad stuff."

She pulls back and wipes her eyes. "Don't be silly. We shouldn't brush it under the carpet. I just hate seeing you torture yourself. You look amazing today and you shouldn't hide away. Stand tall and be proud of who you are and how incredible you look."

I smile. "Thank you. I love you."

"Where the fuck have you been?" yells Grim, marching towards us.

Mum exchanges a concerned look with me. "I got the tube," I snap.

"And you couldn't answer your phone and tell me that? I was worried out of my mind!"

Mum stands. "Well, she's here now, and she's fine as you can see, so take a breath."

"You can't run off like that!" he barks, ignoring Mum.

"You seem to like it when Meli does it," I mutter.

Mum winces. "I think I'll head inside," she says, then rushes back towards the clubhouse.

"What's that supposed to mean?" he growls.

I stand. "You like the way she runs off, the way she pushes your buttons. You like how she dresses and the amount of skin she shows off." I begin to walk away in the direction of the fields. "You like her. You like Meli."

I hear his heavy footsteps behind me. "Not like that, I don't!" he snaps.

"Bullshit. But you don't tell her she looks like a whore, do you?"

"Because she knows she does."

"I've spent years watching you watch her, your eyes full of lust. Not once have you made her feel like you made me feel just then."

"I'm sorry, I shouldn't have said that."

I turn off in the direction of a cluster of trees. "But you did say it. Do you know how much it took for me to put this dress on?"

"Hads, I'm sorry. I don't know what came over me."

"I know you don't look at me like that, but how dare you mock the men who do. Why shouldn't I feel nice? Why can't a man tell me he wants to take me out on a date? Am I that repulsive?" I spin to face him as we step amongst the trees. "I looked nice today. I looked good." He nods. "I can wear what I want!" I feel more empowered by each outburst.

Suddenly, Grim pushes his face close to mine. "I was jealous." I stare wide-eyed at his unexpected confession. "Seeing you in there today was like watching a stranger. You owned him, a powerful man like that, and he did exactly what you wanted. Fuck, it turned me on. But I didn't like the flirting. That pissed me off." I open and close my mouth a couple of times. "And I shouldn't have said it. I knew the second it left my mouth it was a dickish move, but it fell out and you ran off. I'm sorry. You do look amazing and—"

I crash my mouth against his. It's an unplanned and rushed move that makes our teeth clash together in a hungry yet haphazard kiss. And then, as we slow down, his hands cup my face and his tongue sweeps gently against my own. I grip his large shoulders to steady myself, hardly daring to believe that Grim is finally kissing me. He's kissing me!

After a few seconds, he carefully pulls back and stares at me in shock. "We kissed," he whispers, and I nod. "I just kissed my President's little sister." I see the panic in his eyes and I desperately want to rewind to moments ago so we can just kiss over and over and not do the talking part. The teenager in me is stamping her feet and screaming at him not to ruin this moment, this special moment that I've waited over a decade for.

The buzzing of his mobile breaks the silence. "Sorry," he mutters, pulling it out and answering. "Pres?"

GRIM

Fuck, fuck, shitting fuck! What the hell just happened? I turn my back on Hadley and try to focus on Mav's words. "Nick Cambridge has been discharged from hospital. I'm waiting on Hadley to see if she got the paperwork."

"Erm . . . yes, yes, she did. It's right here. I'll get her to come and see you."

"Christ, I've been pacing the office waiting for her call. Tell her to get a damn move on. This is time critical."

I disconnect. "Mav wants the paperwork. Cambridge has been discharged."

"Right. Okay." She squares her shoulders and begins to walk away. Something inside me aches, and I find myself reaching for her and turning her to face me.

"We'll talk about this," I say. "We should talk about it."

She nods, then pulls free and heads back towards the clubhouse.

I see two of everything—two of Ghost, two of Nelly. Good. It's the numb feeling I want. "Another," I mutter, shoving my glass towards Nelly, and she fills it.

"You look like a bundle of happy," she observes.

"Top of the world," I mumble.

"What's bothering you, brother?" asks Ghost.

I tap the side of my head. "In here."

"Drinking won't help," he answers.

"I'm the VP, I can do what I want."

He holds up his arms and shrugs. "Fine."

As I stumble to my bedroom later that night, I feel a hand on my arm and spin to find Meli, smiling that cute smile of hers. "You look lost."

"I'm . . . erm . . ." I look around. Next to me is Hadley's closed bedroom door, and I frown. It's not my room.

"I'll show you," Meli offers, taking my hand and pulling me away, leading me to the next flight of stairs. We stop outside mine. "Are you going to invite me in?" Before I answer, she pushes the door and goes inside. "You've been avoiding me."

"Not avoiding," I mumble.

"Why are you so hung up about it? It's not like it's serious or anything. You overthink everything."

Meli pulls at my belt. I watch her hands tug at the button on my jeans and I come to my senses. I place my hand over hers to stop her trying to eagerly undress me. "No, Meli. We can't."

"I'm sure it'll be fine. Give me a minute to wake it up," she says, winking.

I shake my head and pull her hands from me. "No. We can't."

She rolls her eyes. "You really are getting boring, Grim. I thought hooking up was your speciality?" She stomps out, and I fall on my bed. Staring up at the ceiling, it suddenly hits me hard.

Fuck, I like Hadley!

CHAPTER SEVEN

HADLEY

"Why are you looking so smug?" asks Meli, taking a seat beside me at the breakfast table.

I press my lips together. I've spent the night thinking about Grim and that kiss. "No reason."

"You were serious about the new wardrobe," she adds, nodding at my chosen outfit for the day. I run my hand over the knee-length pencil skirt. I teamed it with the white silk blouse the shop assistant suggested, and she was right, it looks great together. "You look good, like a power-hungry businesswoman."

I smile. "I feel great, actually."

"I'm glad, but it still doesn't explain the smile on your face."

"Maybe it's just a good day to be alive."

We look round as Grim stumbles in, looking terrible. Mav frowns, watching closely as Grim slumps into a chair and blindly feels around for a coffee pot. "What a fucking mess," Meli whispers in disgust. She's never really liked Grim and doesn't bother to hide it.

"What's wrong with him?" I ask casually.

"Lord only knows. He probably got drunk and found a random whore to take to his bed."

I swallow hard, watching Grim from under my eyelashes. "He seems strange lately, don't you think?"

She scowls. "No, I think he's just as annoying as always."

"Maybe something's bothering him?"

"You know your problem, Hads? You spend too much time worrying about the men here. They're big enough and ugly enough to watch themselves. And some brothers, there's just no helping. Grim is a mess of depression and confusion. And I know you used to like him, but seriously, he's not the same guy he once was. He doesn't care about anybody but himself."

"Still, he's Mav's friend, and I'm worried."

Meli rolls her eyes. "You're always worried. Get a new hobby." She flounces out the room without a look back, and Faith fills her spot.

"Have you been back to see Carol?" she whispers.

I shake my head. "It's impossible now because we have to take one of the guys with us."

"Aren't you at work today?" she asks, and I nod. "Then can't you slip out? The guys aren't going to spend the day camped outside your office. They'll drop you and collect, right?" I nod. "So, go and see her. I keep thinking about her and wondering if she's okay. Maybe she just needed food and to see the place cleaned up."

I smile. "If only addiction was so easy to overcome. But I can maybe go and see her, put your mind at rest." She smiles, and I add, "It's sweet you thought about her."

Faith was right. Ghost drops me at the office on the promise I'll call him if I need to go out for anything. I spend the morning working on Harriett's divorce, and at noon I tell Amanda, my boss, I'm nipping out for lunch. She doesn't bat an eyelid as I slip out. Hailing a cab, I head straight for Carol's place. It's not far from where I work, but I don't want to risk the guys seeing me out and about.

For once, Carol's front door is closed. I push it and it's not locked but it's a hopeful sign. There's no clutter on the floor, and I smile as I pass the almost tidy kitchen and head for the living room. I'm unprepared for the sight of Carol lifeless in her chair. She's half-naked with a needle hanging from her arm. Dropping my bag, I rush to her side, gently shaking her. When she doesn't respond, I press a shaky hand to the pulse point on her neck. There's a very faint heartbeat, and I almost sob with joy. I call an ambulance and follow the call handler's instructions to place Carol in the recovery position. Next, I call Mav.

"What's up, little sis?" he answers.

"Confession time," I begin, and he groans. "I'm with Carol, Grim's mum. She's not well, and I'm waiting for an ambulance. Can you meet me at the hospital?"

"Hold the fuck up!" he snaps. "Why the hell are you with her?"

"Long story. Meet me there." I disconnect and check Carol's pulse again, relieved when I still feel it.

○○

By the time the paramedics get Carol stable in the ambulance and get her to hospital, Mav is already waiting for me. He glares at me angrily as I head towards him. "Have you told Grim?" I ask.

"No, I haven't. What would I say?"

"He's been to see her recently," I mutter. "He knows she's using."

"But he doesn't know you're interfering, does he?" Mav growls, and I shake my head. "He's dealing with shit right now, half of which I think is down to Carol, and now, you're meddling in crap that's nothing to do with you. What are you playing at?"

"I just wanted to help. He mentioned her, and I didn't know he was seeing her, so I went to the house. I was hoping she was clean, that I could talk to her about Grim, maybe help reunite them."

Mav rolls his eyes. "And how's that working out?"

I glance at Carol as they push her trolley past us. "Actually, not so good."

"No shit. Christ, Hadley, I know you want to be Mother fucking Teresa, but sometimes you make things worse." He marches inside, and I stare after him, stung by his words.

GRIM

The call from Maverick was unexpected, and when I arrive at the hospital just after my liquid lunch, I can't see straight. Mav grips my arm and stares at me. "Are you drunk?"

"I skipped lunch and opted for whiskey," I mutter.

"It's not even one o'clock!" he snaps. "Hadley, get him a black coffee!"

"Hadley's here?" I ask, confused.

Mav takes me into the relatives' room. It's the same room I sat in when Dad passed, so I'm already expecting the worst. "Is she dead?"

Mav shakes his head. "They're pumping her stomach, but it doesn't look good, brother."

Hadley returns and passes me the coffee. "You didn't need to leave work, Hadley," I mumble, secretly grateful she's here. "I'll be fine."

She looks at Mav with a guilty expression. "Actually, I found her."

"Where?"

The door opens and a doctor enters. "Which one of you is the relative?"

"Me." I hand the coffee back to Hadley and follow him outside the room.

"Your mother is going to be okay," he says, and I'm surprised at the mixed emotions I feel. "She's sleeping, and I expect she'll stay like that for a few more hours, but by tomorrow she'll be able to go home. There's a drug programme we can refer her for, however, the waiting list is long."

I shake my head. I've heard it all before. "She's not ready," I say. "What's the point if she's not ready?"

"I'll take you to see her," he adds, not bothering to argue with me.

Mum's complexion is pale and dirty. The nurse offers to give her a bed bath, and I agree, stepping behind the curtain while she gets to work. Afterwards, I take a seat by her bed and watch her sleep. It reminds me of when I was a kid and I'd watch her chest move up and down to make sure she wasn't dead. I shake my head in disgust, remembering I must have only been three years old.

The curtain slides back and Hadley comes in. My heart squeezes. Just being around her makes things feel better. "Hey, how is she?"

"She can come home tomorrow."

"Great news. I'm pleased. Will she be coming home to the clubhouse?" she asks.

I shake my head. She'll hate that and only run the second she gets a chance. "Where did you say you found her?"

"Oh . . . about that . . . I was at her house."

I frown. "What?"

"I was visiting Carol to check on her."

"Why?"

"Because I wanted to get her well again. You have so many unanswered questions about your childhood, and you deserve to know the answers. And if she can get better, you deserve to have a mum in your life."

"You cleaned up the house?" I whisper, and she nods. "You took her food?" She nods again. I can't describe the disappointment I feel finding out it wasn't Mum getting well but Hadley interfering. "I thought she was getting better."

"I wanted to help. I'm sorry."

"I saw a glimmer of hope that maybe she was starting to wake up and get clean."

"I was going to tell you," she begins, but I hold my hand up to stop her.

"Get out."

"Grim, please—"

"Get out!" I roar, and she jumps in fright. The nurse rushes over. "I want her to leave," I snap, and she ushers Hadley from the room.

I stare down at Mum's pale face. "Somehow, even when you don't know it, you let me down. I can't deal with it anymore. Dad was right, you're a lost cause, and I can't be around you anymore because you're sucking the life out of me."

I leave the hospital and head for the nearest bar.

HADLEY

My mobile buzzes loudly on my nightstand. I feel around for it and press it to my ear. "Huh?"

"So, about earlier," slurs Grim.

I frown and sit up, glancing at the time. "It's three in the morning, Grim. Is everything okay?"

"How upset are you that I yelled?"

"You never call me. What's wrong?"

"I'm in a bit of a tight pickle." He begins to laugh, and I hear another voice telling him to hurry up. "It seems it's illegal to drink and drive," he says in a conspiring tone, "and the nice policeman caught me. I need a solicitor to come to the station once I'm sober, for interview."

"You got yourself arrested?"

"Yes. I also would like to point out that they're a little heavy handed when it comes to making an arrest. My ego is bruised."

"Jesus, Grim. I'll be there."

"Thanks, little one, I owe you."

I don't sleep for the rest of the night, tossing and turning and thinking about Grim. By morning, I'm exhausted. I knock on Mav's office door, and he glances up. "Grim got himself arrested."

"What?"

"He called. He needs legal representation."

"Do you want to do it?"

I nod. "I owe him after meddling in his life."

Mav sighs. "You were trying to help, Hads. He knows that. He just gets weird when the club knows his business."

"Do I need an escort?"

He grabs his keys, and states, "I'd be happy to take you."

I sit patiently in the interviewing room at the police station. When the door finally opens and Grim enters, I arch a surprised brow. "How the hell did you get in that state?"

He cocks a bruised eyebrow and grins. "Not sure."

"Did the police do that, or did you get into a fight?" I grip his chin and turn his head from side to side to inspect the cuts and bruises on his face.

"All me, I think. Look, thanks for coming."

I glare at the police officer standing in the doorway. "Take his cuffs off," I order, and he does. Grim takes a seat, and the officer steps out of the room. "Drunk driving?" I snap, and Grim shrugs.

"If it helps, I don't remember."

"I suggest you come up with a good explanation. The judge isn't going to like you as it is, and looking like that's just going to make it worse." I pull out a notepad. "We'll use the shock of your mum," I add, beginning to prepare a statement.

It's three hours later when we leave the police station. Grim's charged with drunk driving, and they'll send him a date to attend court, but it's likely he'll lose his driver's licence as he already has points for speeding. Mav picks us up in the club's car, and I fill him in while Grim sits silently in the back.

"We need to swing by the hospital," Mav eventually announces. "Carol is coming to the clubhouse."

"What?" asks Grim, leaning forward. It's the first sign of life he's shown in hours. "Why?"

"Because she needs our help. I spoke to Mama B, and she made the decision. She's gonna help her to recover with Doc's help."

"She's a fucking addict, Mav. You can't undo years of damage. This isn't a film where we lock her in a room for a day and she comes out cured!"

"You think I don't know that?" asks Mav, stopping outside the hospital, and we all get out of the car.

Grim grips his head and growls to no one in particular. "It's like living with the Brady Bunch," he complains. "This never-ending need to help the world become a better place is bullshit!" Mav smirks, and it only annoys Grim more. "You remember who we are, right?"

"Remind me," says Mav, leaning against the car, folding his arms over his chest.

"You're the kid who killed his mother's one true love. I'm the kid who stuck a knife in his mother's lover without flinching. I watched him gargle on his own blood and didn't bat an eyelid. We take life, we don't save it. I get a kick from watching it drain from a man's eyes. It gets me fucking hard knowing I can do that without feeling a thing!"

"We save lives too. We saved Rylee, Faith, Maddi, and Gracie, and we can save your mum. If we don't try, we'll regret it."

"I won't," says Grim coldly. "Yesterday, when the doc told me she was gonna be okay, I was upset. Upset it wasn't finally over. Because I need it to be over now, I can't look out for her anymore."

Mav slaps him on the shoulder. "I hear you, Grim, I do. You're struggling right now, so I'll deal with Carol. I'm not asking you to sit with her or even check in with her. But I can't walk away and pretend she was never part of this club. Your dad wouldn't want me to."

Grim sighs before getting back in the car, and Mav turns to me. "Stay with him. He needs us."

I climb in the back beside him. Carol can sit up front, away from Grim. "I'm always here," I begin, watching out the window. "If you need to talk."

"Nothing can ever happen between us," he says firmly. "Ever. We're not the same. You're a good girl, and I'm fucked up. You're too young for me and you're Mav's little sister. I don't look at you in that way and I never will. I just want to be perfectly clear, we're never gonna happen."

I continue to stare out the window, scared to look in his direction in case my expression gives my pain away. "Totally, we're not like that at all, and I'm definitely not into you."

"Good. Let's just avoid each other from now on and make it easier."

"You called me," I mutter.

"I know. I needed your help, and you were great in there, really professional. Thanks."

"But now you don't need my help, you want me to stay the hell away from you?"

"It's for the best," he mumbles.

I scoff. Best for who? The ache in my chest is too much and I rub the spot. "I need some air." I get out the car and lean against the door. The urge to get away from Grim is overwhelming, and I find myself walking away from the car and out of the parking lot. Needing to clear my head, I head for the river just over the road.

CHAPTER EIGHT

GRIM

"You just let her go?" snaps Mav, looking around frantically.

"She said she felt ill and needed air. I didn't notice until she'd already gone." Mum sits quietly in the front seat, her head bowed. "Yah know what, I'll go and find her. You take your latest rescue mission home." I get out the car and head in the same direction as Hadley.

I don't have to walk far before I spot her sitting on the steps leading down to the river. "You shouldn't just leave like that," I say, joining her. "We spoke about this before."

"I'm fine. I'll meet you back at the clubhouse." "Not gonna happen."

"You should be with your mum."

"I think Mav has it covered," I mutter bitterly.

"He's right, your dad would have made the club help her."

"Bullshit," I snap. "He never helped her when he was around. He told me she didn't want help, and you can't help an addict until they admit they need it. Well, she never has and she never will."

"If you're so against us helping, why were you visiting her?"

I stare out over the river. "Guilt."

"For?"

"Killing her boyfriend when I was thirteen."

"Someone told me about that," she says thoughtfully. "Why did you kill him?"

"He was a dick. That particular day, I was visiting for the weekend, he was laying into her and I'd had it. I wanted to make sure he didn't do that when I wasn't around to protect her. Not that she was happy about it. In fact, she was really mad. I think that's where we started to drift apart."

Hadley takes a deep breath and releases it slowly. "Look, I know sometimes Mav can be annoying, but most of the time, his decisions make sense. He's doing this because it's the right thing to do."

"I was thinking of hitting the road again," I announce. "But after today, there's no chance of that happening, is there?"

She shakes her head. "No. You'll lose your licence for a while."

I stand and hold my hand out to her. She takes it, and I pull her up too. "Then I guess I'd better go and listen to Mav's crazy plan to save my mum and work out how I can help."

We take a slow walk in the direction of the clubhouse. "I'm sorry for being so harsh back there, Hadley, but you know I'm talking sense."

"Forget about it."

"I just want you to know I—"

"Grim, please, just forget it."

I nod. Whatever it is I'm feeling, it's not real. I don't see Hadley in that way and the only explanation I have right now is that my head is a mess. I need to put distance between us to get everything straight. She'll understand that in the end, it's for the best.

The first night having Mum back isn't so bad. She's still very tired from her hospital stay, and Doc managed to sort her a programme for the controlled drug, methadone. It should ease her from the heroin gradually, and over time, he plans to reduce the methadone until she's clean. He made it sound so easy, even I felt hopeful, but as I watch her tossing and turning in her sleep, something tells me I'm kidding myself.

Mav sticks his head in. "How's she doing?"

I nod. "Seems okay. She's sleeping a lot."

"I just went to see Harriett. She's looking much better too. I think she'll be up and about soon."

"Good news. Heard anything about her husband?"

He shakes his head. "Arthur's keeping him sweet right now, but it won't last. He'll want revenge."

"We need to get in there first.""Arthur asked if we want in on the casino jobs."

"Not really our scene, is it?"

"No. Once the job's pulled off, maybe his attention will be on that instead of Harriett. Fancy a drink downstairs?"

I stare at Mum for a minute before nodding. She isn't going anywhere. There're no windows in this room and the door will be locked.

Downstairs, the bar is quiet. Hadley is in the corner reading a book, and Ghost is watching football on the large screen. Nelly hands us each a beer, and we take a seat. My eyes occasionally drift to Hadley. "Drunk driving," says Mav, shaking his head. "What the fuck, Grim?"

"I don't know what I was thinking," I mutter.

"Clearly, you weren't."

I bury my face in my hands. "It's this place, Mav. Being here, seeing Mum, remembering the shit that went down, learning about Meli and noticing . . ." I trail off before I say Hadley's name, but my eyes fix on her again.

"She's been there for you a lot these last few weeks."

"Huh?"

"Hads." I keep quiet, not trusting myself to speak. "I noticed you've spent some time together, but the real tell-tale sign was when she thanked me for the several hundred pounds' worth of clothes I apparently paid for." He laughs. "I know you said you'd taken her shopping, but that's quite some bill."

"I just wanted to treat her, to say thanks for listening."

"You don't have to explain to me. The question is, why did you lie to her?"

I shrug. "I thought she might see it as something else."

"You thought she'd see the truth." When I don't reply, he leans closer. "Maybe you're having trouble seeing it yourself?"

I smile sadly. "I see it, brother. Trust me, I see it."

"Yet you're holding back."

"This is Hadley we're talking about," I whisper. "Your sister. She deserves better."

"Better than my most trusted brother? The man who'd lay his life down for me? Man, you're my VP, I can't think of anyone else I'd rather have looking after her."

I stare at him, shocked at his confession. "I'm also the guy who shared women with you. The guy who hooked up with random women night after night."

"So, what, you'll never settle down because of your past? We were young, it's what young lads do. But we're getting older now, and you should be thinking of settling."

"See," I say, sitting straighter, "it's that right there. I'm not the type to settle, and you know I'm not. I'll hurt her because she is that type."

"Why have you always gotta overthink everything, Grim? Just give it a shot and see how it plays out. You could surprise yourself."

I shake my head, taking a pull on my beer. "I expected better from you," I mutter. "Find a decent man for your sister."

He smirks. "I already have."

HADLEY

Two days pass and I can't lift my mood. Grim is avoiding me, and it's so obvious, it's embarrassing. If I enter a room he's in, he leaves within minutes. His mum is struggling, which is having an impact on him. He looks pale and exhausted, and I desperately want to check in with him. Rylee sits beside me on the couch, and I look up from the book I'm pretending to read. "So, Grim is outside his mum's room. She's banging on the door and crying, and he's struggling to hold it together."

My heart squeezes. "Poor Grim."

"I thought . . . well, actually, Mav thought you could go and speak to him, try and get him to rest."

I shake my head. "He won't listen to me, Rylee."

She takes my hand and smiles gently. "He will, Hads. He's in need of a woman who's patient and calm, and you're perfect for that." Mav is watching from his office doorway. "Do it for Mav," she adds, and I sigh. "Thanks, Hadley."

I hear Carol the second I climb the stairs. Grim is outside her room, leaning against the door with his eyes squeezed shut. I slide down the wall opposite until my arse hits the ground, and Grim opens his eyes. A look passes over his expression that tells me he's relieved to see me, and it's the boost I need. "You look terrible," I say.

"Thanks."

"When did you last sleep?" He shrugs. "I had a terrible day in the office. I could do with a nap. Wanna join?" He shakes his head, and my heart sinks. "Okay, then how about you take ten minutes out? Come sit with me and have a break?"

He eventually nods, and I smile. Pushing to stand, I wait for him to do the same. He follows me down a flight of stairs to my room. I keep the lights low and open the large window to allow a cool breeze to blow through. "Take a seat," I say, pointing to the bed. He sits down with his head hanging and his shoulders slumped. It breaks my heart to see him like this. "Relax," I whisper, carefully moving towards him and sliding my hands over his shoulders. I slip his kutte from his big arms and lay it beside him on the bed, then I massage his shoulders. He groans, letting his head fall back.

"Lie down, I'm good at massage," I offer. He hesitates, staring into my eyes. "Let me look after you, Grim." He nods, gripping his T-shirt and pulling it over his head. I try not to gasp at his toned chest as he kicks off his boots and lays on his stomach. Rubbing my hands together to warm them up, I stare in awe at the way his shoulders bunch and his back looks so manly. I kneel on the bed beside him and begin to work the muscles in his shoulders. He groans with pleasure, and it does things to my insides. Without thinking, I throw my leg over him and work my hands up and down his tense back.

It's not long before I hear his light snores and I'm smiling to myself. I watch my hands glide over his skin a final time, then slowly lay my body over his. He's so warm and inviting, I'm tempted to drift off, but the thought of him finding me like this makes me get up. Instead, I sit beside him, leaning my back against the wall. His head is facing towards me, resting on his crossed arms. He looks so peaceful. I lie down on my front and mimic his position, watching him sleep. I wish I could spend the rest of my life exactly like this.

GRIM

"You fucking killed him," Ma screams, staring at Mark's still body. Right at that moment, the door opens and Dad stalks in like a big, angry bear. He also stares at the lifeless body, then at my bloodied hand still gripping the knife.

"Ah, shit, Grim, couldn't you just punch the guy?"

"I did," I argue.

"Maybe next time, don't pull the knife first?"

It's easier said than done. Sometimes, I don't know it's in my hand, it's almost like a natural extension. Copper steps in behind Dad and also groans. "I'll call the clean-up crew."

I tuck my knife away as Dad helps Ma to stand. "You couldn't stay sober just for a few days?" he growls.

"This is not my fault," she hisses. "It's yours for dumping him on me." She narrows her eyes in my direction. "Just so you can go and fuck your whores." "Oh, baby, trust me, I don't need to dump him on you for that. He's your kid too, and I stupidly thought you'd want to see him."

"He's just killed the love of my life," she wails, and Dad slams a hand over her mouth to shut her up. When he uncovers it, she looks at me with such hate, I want to shrivel up. "I never want to see you again. I hate you."

─────

My eyes shoot open, and I suck in a breath. Why the fuck do my dreams all go back to that day? Hadley is beside me, sleeping peacefully. I relax as I watch her, wondering what she dreams about. She's fully clothed, lying on top of the sheets, and I allow my eyes to run down her body. I've missed her so much these last few days, and when she came to help me earlier tonight, it was a relief.

I carefully tuck her hair behind her ear, and she jumps in fright. She opens her eyes but relaxes the second she sees me. "Sorry," I whisper.

"You slept," she murmurs, glancing at her watch. "At least three hours."

"New record," I joke. "Thanks for making me take a break."

"I'm here anytime you need me, Grim."

I run my finger along her jaw. "Why are you so nice to me all the time?"

She props her head up to rest on her hand and uses her other hand to interlock her fingers with mine. "It's what friends are for," she whispers, staring at the way my hand grips hers.

I turn on my side too and prop my head on my free hand. "I've missed being around you these last few days."

"Me too."

I push her hand back until it lands on the pillow, and she naturally rolls on her back. I hover above her, both of us watching each other, waiting for the other to make a move. "Let's not do that again," I whisper. "Avoid one another."

"Agreed."

I move my head towards her, slow enough for her to move if she doesn't want this. When it's clear she's not going anywhere, I gently place a kiss on her lips. It's brief, but I'm not done. I'm just giving her another chance to push me away. "This could be dangerous," I whisper against her lips.

"I hope so."

Our mouths clash together, and this time, a fire burns deep inside me. It's like a hunger, and the only way to feed it is to take everything she's giving me. Her fingers run through my hair, occasionally gripping it at the roots. When she wraps her leg around my thigh and pushes me to lie back, I take her with me so that she's on top, kissing me like I'm everything she's ever wanted. It feels fucking amazing.

CHAPTER NINE

HADLEY

I'm not experienced when it comes to men. I'm not a virgin, but I haven't slept with lots of guys like some of the other women here. It was just one guy when I was in college. He'd spent years bullying me, shoving me so I'd knock into people or fall, just childish stuff. I got invited to a party and ended up alone in a bedroom with him. He confessed he was awful to me because he really liked me, so I slept with him. Not because I wanted to, particularly, but because I wanted him to stop being a dick. It didn't work. He was still a dick, and the sex wasn't even worth it. It was terrible. It felt nothing like this! This is causing a raw need to build in the pit of my stomach, and the only man to soothe it is Grim.

Straddling him, I can feel his erection prodding me. It's difficult to ignore when it feels hard enough to bust out of his jeans. I grind against him, and he groans. I love that sound, so I break the kiss and smile. We're both panting. I sit up and lift my top over my head. The fear of him seeing my body seems to have left the building, because as his bright blue eyes watch me, I feel brazen enough to remove my bra. I continue to grind against him, and he hisses. His hands run up my ribs, to my breasts, then his thumbs lightly brush my nipples, and I close my eyes, continuing to move against his erection.

"Are we really doing this?" he pants.

"We better be," I answer with a nervous laugh.

He grins, then grips my waist and flips me back down on the bed. Kneeling between my legs, undoing his belt while watching me, he unzips his jeans and pushes them down his thighs. Taking his wallet from his back pocket, he removes a condom and places it on the bed. "This could change everything," he warns, running his hands up and down my thighs.

"It's too late now. We've already gone too far to turn back."

He hooks his fingers in my leggings and pulls them down with my underwear. He throws them to the floor and goes back to staring at me. I feel myself blushing, wondering what the hell he must be thinking. Then, he surprises me by bending his face down between my legs and pushing his hands under my arse. He lifts me to meet his mouth, and I almost scream in shock when he pushes his tongue against my pussy like he's eating a meal. My embarrassment is soon forgotten as that heat builds from deep inside. His tongue presses against my clit, rubbing vigorously, then he pushes a finger inside, hooking it slightly and making my entire body jerk with pleasure.

"Fuck, you taste good," he pants, sucking my clit into his mouth. My fingers dig into his scalp, bringing him closer as the sensation reaches on a new level. I'm so far gone, I don't care that I'm shamelessly grinding against his mouth.

I see white spots at the back of my eyes and my entire body begins to convulse in a way it's never done before. I don't know if I should cry or scream as a warm wave of deliciousness washes over me, relaxing me instantly. "I've never seen anything so hot in my life," whispers Grim, positioning himself on his knees between my legs. "Are you sure about this, Hads?" I nod, unable to find words through the brain fog I'm currently experiencing. His cock pushes at my entrance, and he grips my thighs as he slowly eases in an inch at a time. I feel myself stretching to accommodate him, and those dull flickers of buzzing energy begin to dart around again.

Once he's fully inside, Grim leans over me, a hand either side of my head. "There's no going back now, not after this." I make a mumbling sound, and he smiles. "You understand, Hadley? This is it now, me and you." I groan as he withdraws and grab onto his shoulders as he slams into me, taking my breath away. "Say it," he whispers in my ear. "Say you're mine."

I stare up at his eyes, which seem bluer somehow. "I'm yours," I pant out, and I stop myself from adding 'I always have been'.

He bends my leg and turns me onto my side, wrapping it around his waist as he continues to fuck me. I feel him so much deeper like this, and it takes only seconds for me to reach another orgasm. He then flips me onto my front and enters me from behind, gripping my hips and slamming into me fast. "Fuck, you feel too good," he mutters. "Tell me you're on the pill."

I nod, noticing the unused condom on the bed beside us. "Yes."

"Thank fuck!" He releases into me. He pushes one last time, then lets out a relaxed groan and flops down beside me. He hooks his arm around me and pulls me to his side, tucking me against him and throwing a leg over me. "You're fucking hot."

I smile. "You're not so bad yourself."

We drift to sleep naked and wrapped in each other.

I woke twice in the night to check he hadn't realised the mistake he'd made and left, but he was still wrapped around me each time. So, when it's time to actually get up and Grim wakes me with his mouth attached to my breast, it puts a smile on my lips. "I thought you'd do a midnight flit," I say.

He parts my legs and settles between them. "I told you last night, this changes everything." He slides into me with ease, and I close my eyes in pleasure. "It took me too long to wake up."

"I'm glad you did."

By the time we've showered and get downstairs, breakfast is over, and Brea is cleaning up the kitchen. She smiles and greets us. "Morning, I'll get you some eggs."

"Actually, I'm gonna talk to Mav," says Grim, winking at me. "I'll catch up with you later."

Mum smirks at me as he leaves. "What?" I ask innocently.

"Don't give me that look, young lady. I have Irish blood, so I know when Cupid's been at work."

I laugh, rolling my eyes. "You're seeing things."

"You're everything he needs," she says warmly, and I smile wider. "Just be careful."

"We haven't really put a label on anything, so can you keep it to yourself for a while? Just while we figure out what's happening?" She nods. "Thanks, Mum."

GRIM

Hadley. Fuck. Hadley. I shake my head in disbelief. I told her I was seeing Mav, but in truth, I needed a minute to process the last twenty-four hours. I slide down the oak tree and rest my head back against the rough bark. It's hard to believe I finally listened to my heart for once and it felt right. I feel good when I'm around her. It's like whenever she's near, there's a light of hope in my fucking pointless life.

I tried to leave her alone, because fuck knows I don't wanna be the reason her light ever fades, but she made it too hard. Being the selfish prick that I am, it didn't take much convincing to make her mine. I mean, I actually said those fucking words out loud, and I didn't feel panic or dread. But then, I think about Meli and how she's going to react to this, and I get this sick feeling in the pit of my stomach.

I should have told Hadley from the beginning, but I talked myself out of it time and time again because what was the point if nothing was happening between any of us? Meli and I were nothing more than a quick fuck when there was no one else around to turn to, and Hadley, well, she wasn't supposed to mean anything to me. Turns out, she means everything. I groan out loud and jump in fright when Hadley appears. "That was a loaded groan," she states.

"Sorry, I'm overthinking."

"Any regrets?" she asks, her voice full of dread. I smile and hold my hand out to her. She takes it, and I tug her to sit with me.

"No, Hads. No fucking regrets at all. In fact, I wanna tell the world about us and I'm trying to talk myself into slowing down."

"Well, Mama B kind of guessed, but I asked her to keep it to herself for now."

"I just . . . well, with my reputation, I know the guys are gonna be worried for you, and the ol' ladies will warn you off. I don't want anyone to ruin it."

"I know what you mean," she mutters. "Meli is gonna overreact."

"Meli?" I repeat, "Why?"

"You know how she feels about you."

Panic fills me. "Huh?"

She smirks. "She can't stand you, Grim. You know she can't. She's gonna have a thing or two to say for sure."

"I don't blame them, any of them, they're right to worry for you."

She rests her head on my shoulder, and I kiss it gently. "I'm not worried, Grim. Did you talk to Maverick?"

I shake my head. "No. I needed five minutes, but he's my next stop. He kind of pushed me towards you the other night."

She looks up, surprised. "He did?"

"I think he worked it out that I liked you. He told me to go for it, said he couldn't imagine anyone better for his sister."

Hadley grins. "That's actually cute."

"Don't let him hear you say that." I spot Meli heading our way, and I stand. "That's my cue to leave."

"Just for the record, I'm not going to tell her yet. I want to enjoy this for a few more days."

I nod in agreement. I need to speak to Meli alone before this gets out, but now isn't the right time. "Catch you later," I say.

As I head in, Meli narrows her eyes. "You two look cosy," she whispers.

"She's been a great friend, Meli. Nothing more."

I find Mav in the kitchen making coffee. "Don't we have people who do that for you?" I ask, grinning. He hates to be treated like he's superior around here and wouldn't dream of asking anyone to get his coffee, but I love to wind him up.

"Did you get some sleep last night?" he asks, arching his brow suggestively.

"Huh?"

"Rylee asked Hadley to force you to rest. That's the last we saw of either of you."

I roll my eyes. "Should have known."

"We were worried, brother."

"Actually, your little plan worked. We talked and . . . well, that's all you need to know. But we're not ready for the club to find out. We're taking it slow."

"Good for you."

"Aren't you worried?" I ask, irritated by his easy attitude.

"Why would I be?"

"Because she's your sister, Mav. Look at my track record."

He holds his coffee and leans against the kitchen worktop. "First of all, you're both adults. Hadley might be quiet and laid back, but she'll let you know about it if you mess this up. But I'm not worried, Grim, because she's gonna be good for you. She's what you need, and as soon as you see that, you'll do anything to keep her."

HADLEY

"Spill the truth," demands Meli, standing before me with her hands on her hips.

I laugh. "Who the hell are you, the Queen?"

"You're spending a lot of time with Grim. All the club girls are talking about it. Star and Skye are his favourite girls and even they haven't seen anything of him lately."

I try to hide my smile. "I don't know what to tell you, Meli. He's having a tough time, and I'm there for him. I'm being a good friend."

"Guys like Grim don't have friends. He has fuck buddies, one-night stands, and a bottle of whiskey under his bed for when he's exhausted all of the above."

My smile falters. "You're overreacting."

"I just want to check he's not taking advantage of my sister."

"Well, I can assure you, he isn't. You seem to forget we're twins, Meli, and we're both adults."

"You're being extremely defensive."

Rolling my eyes, I push to stand and march towards the clubhouse. "I'm going to see Harriett. Are you coming?"

Harriett is sitting up in bed holding Ivy, who's sound asleep. I smile. She's just the cutest little baby. "Hey, you look a lot better."

"I feel it," she whispers.

Ghost shifts in the corner, and I jump in fright. "Jesus, Ghost, what are you doing there?"

"Keeping Harriett company."

"You shouldn't be hiding in corners, it's weird," says Meli.

Ghost smiles. "It's all in the name, sweet pea. I'll let you girls catch up. Call if you need anything," he says to Harriett, giving her a parting wink.

"He seems very keen," says Meli, taking a seat.

"He's been so nice to me," says Harriett.

"I bet he has," mutters Meli, quipping a brow.

"Can you give it a rest?" I tell Harriett, "She's anti-men right now. I think she's spent too much time with Rosey."

"If you ask me, she's got the right idea. Kill the bastards, and we're all free," states Meli.I laugh, and Harriett suppresses a smile. "Shit, next you'll be burning your bra in the backyard."

Meli puts her hands on her hips again. "Well, they take what they want and then brush you off without an explanation. They don't give a crap that you're left with shit to deal with."

"Meli, we're supposed to cheer Harriett up. What's gotten into you?"

"Am I right, H?" asks Meli. "You must want to see your ex dead after everything."

Harriett stares down at baby Ivy. "I just want him to leave me alone."

"Some men don't listen, though, do they? I'm sure with all the money he has, he'll fight you every step of the way."

"Fuck, Meli," I snap angrily, and she blinks innocently. "Shut the hell up, will yah? And, actually, he was served the restraining order and the divorce papers and took the news very well."

"Like Rylee's ex did?"

"Rylee's ex?" repeats Harriett.

"Ignore her," I mutter. "He was a head case, Meli, you can't use him as an example."

"What happened with Rylee's ex?" asks Harriett again, sounding more alarmed.

"He raided this place, got her on her own, and scared the crap out of her. He wanted her to know he could still get to her!"

"Meli!" I yell, and the baby begins to cry. Ghost bursts in, looking concerned. "It's not the same—he was a cop!"

"What's going on?" Ghost barks.

"Meli was talking too much," I mutter.

He stares at Harriett's face. "What did she say?"

"It's fine," Harriett mutters.

"It's not fine. I can see in your face it isn't. Meli, get out."

"What? I didn't do anything. I was just saying—"

"Get out now, or I'll remove you!" he orders, and she huffs before stomping out with Ghost following after her.

I smile awkwardly at Harriett. "Sorry about her. Look, every case is different, and I'm not saying Nick is going to take this lying down cos I don't know him, but I do know he won't get in here. Ghost doesn't leave your side, and the club is much better on security since the whole Rylee thing. But, like I said, he was a cop, and they have powers to gain entry. All you have to do is concentrate on Ivy. We'll do the rest."

I'm lying on my bed when the door opens and Grim comes in. He locks it and begins to strip out of his clothes until he's down to his boxers. I laugh as he slides over me and pulls me to lay against him. "I need to feel you against me," he whispers in my ear.

"Tough day?"

"Mum is screwing. She's a mess. I made the mistake of going in the room today, and she's sweating and agitated. She practically clawed my back to get out of there." He turns slightly, giving me a glimpse of his scratched back.

I wrap my arms around his neck. "Poor you. What did Doc say?"

"The usual, it takes time, she'll get there, blah blah blah."

I smile, running my fingers up and down his back. "He's right, though. These first few weeks will be the toughest."

He kisses me. "As long as I have you here, it'll be fine."

His hands roam my body, unfastening my clothing as he goes. I let him strip me down to my underwear and close my eyes as he gets lost in me.

CHAPTER TEN

GRIM

A week passes and I can't get enough of Hadley. I want to spend every waking moment beside her or inside of her. Either one will do. She's easing everything that's fucked in my life right now. I always thought Hadley would be a prude in the bedroom, yet she's anything but, and as I stare up at her amazing body while she rides me, I'm filled with an overwhelming desire to officially make her mine. It's too soon, I know it is, but it doesn't stop me wanting it . . . wanting her.

She comes apart, interlocking our fingers as she moves faster to chase the feeling. When she collapses over my chest, I grip her around the waist and thrust up into her, needing my own release. "Do you think we'll ever get tired of this?" she whispers.

I throw my arm over my eyes, trying to catch my breath. "I fucking hope not."

"It's been a whole week of sneaking around. We're doing good."

"About that . . . I think we should tell everyone. I was gonna break it to the brothers in church tonight."

She places kisses along my chest. "Whatever you want."

I still her. "What do you want, Hads?"

"For us to stay in our little bubble forever?"

I smile. "You know that can't happen. We just need to get it out there and get the negative comments out the way. Everyone will get used to us."

"Even Meli and Rosey?"

"They hate all men. It wouldn't matter who you were with, they'd have something bad to say. Ignore them both."

I playfully slap her bare arse as I get out of bed. "I'll bring you breakfast in bed seeing as it's the weekend," I offer, and she stretches out, trying to entice me to re-join her. Instead, I kiss her. "Wait here."

Downstairs, everyone is busy talking as I load a plate with enough for two people. I'm almost out of the kitchen when Meli blocks my path. "We need to talk," she says firmly.

"Not now, Meli, I got something to do."

"Something or someone?"

I roll my eyes impatiently. "What do you care?"

"This is important, Grim, and trust me, I'd rather not be in a room talking with you, but it's something you need to know."

I groan impatiently and march towards Mav's office. Once inside, I place the plate down. "Spit it out."

"I'm pregnant."

The world stops turning, everything around me sounds muffled, and I think I stop breathing for a few seconds as I process her words. "No," I mutter, shaking my head. "No, you can't be."

"I know it's not what you want to hear, but I am, so let's save all the dramatics because I don't have the patience for it."

"You . . . you don't understand—"

"I don't want it. I'm having an abortion, but Rosey said I should tell you at least."

Suddenly, I feel sick. "Rosey knows?"

"I needed to talk to someone, and you're never around."

"Who else knows?" I snap.

"No one. Relax, our dirty secret is safe. Look, it's booked for this evening, and providing it goes well, I can be in and out. My only problem is, I need one of you guys to accompany me out, and unless you want another brother knowing my business, it has to be you."

I nod. "Of course."

"Great. Well, be ready for five."

She breezes out of the office like she didn't just drop a big bombshell. Mav comes in seconds later and looks up from his mobile in surprise. "Hey, did you need me?" I shake my head. "Are you okay? You look sick."

"Yeah, I'm fine. Sorry." I grab the plate of food and leave the office, dumping the lot in a nearby bin as I head out of the club.

HADLEY

I'm not sure how long I lie in bed before I realise Grim has probably been dragged on something club-related and he's not bringing me breakfast. I shower, dress, and head downstairs to the normal chaos surrounding the kitchen. "Morning," I say as I sit beside Meli and Rosey. "Anyone seen Grim today?" I ask casually.

They both fix me with a stare. "Why?" they say in unison.

"No reason. I was gonna speak to him about the court case for his drunk driving charge."

"The last time I saw him, he was walking out of here with a plate loaded for two. He's probably in his room with some skank-whore," says Rosey.

"Not all women who sleep with a club member are skanks or whores," I say defensively.

"Please, I'm not in the mood for a speech about how all the men here are good and they just need someone on their side," Meli mutters.

"I get you two didn't have great experiences with some of the men here but they're not all bad."

"Just because you have the hots for Grim," says Rosey, sniggering.

"I do not," I snap. "Grow up. For two women who hate men, you sure hang around here a lot." I leave them to their bitch-fest and go back to my room to call Grim. When he doesn't answer, I send him a text asking if he's okay. He was so happy this morning, and if he filled a plate for breakfast, what stopped him coming back up to me?

I put on the television and opt for a movie day. I'm sure Grim will turn up whenever he's finished what he's doing.

GRIM

A few minutes before five, I send a text to Meli telling her I'm outside. I've spent the day by the river thinking shit through, but my head still feels a mess. When she appears with Rosey, I remove my bike helmet. "She ain't coming," I snap.

"Excuse me, that's not your choice," says Rosey.

"You shouldn't be driving," says Meli. "And I don't think I should come home on the bike after . . ." she trails off.

Rosey smirks and holds up a set of car keys. "I'll drive."

We're quiet on the way to the private clinic. I sit in the back with Meli because the thought of being up front with Rosey makes me shudder. Meli fidgets with her hands, so I place mine over hers, and she smiles gratefully. "Listen," I begin, "are you sure about this?"

"Please don't do that," she begs. "This is the right thing."

"As long as it's the right thing for you, because if it's not, just say and I'll stick by you."

"Me and you?" She shakes her head. "We'd never work."

"I know that, but people co-parent all the time."

Meli laughs. "Can you really see yourself with a kid, Grim?" I shake my head, and she goes on, "Exactly, and neither can I. It wasn't supposed to happen, and I took the morning-after pill, but it must have failed. Let's just get through this and pretend it never happened."

The procedure is short. It took less time to suction the embryo out of Meli than the consultation took when we first arrived. We sit in silence in the recovery room while Meli sips tea and eats a biscuit like this is all normal. "Now what?" I ask.

She pauses mid-bite. "Now, we go home and pretend this never happened."

"Just like that?"

"What do you want me to say, Grim? It's done, and we can go on with our lives."

I nod. "Fine. Are you gonna tell Hadley?"

She eyes me suspiciously. "I wasn't planning to, but since we're on the subject, I wanted to speak to you about her." I hold my breath, waiting for her to ask the question. "I want you to stay away from her."

I frown, not expecting her to say that. "What?"

"I know she's helped you through the last few weeks, but I don't want you getting any ideas. She's not like me—she'll fall for you, and she'll end up hurt."

"Hadley's an adult," I mutter.

"She's my twin sister, Grim. If you ever went there with her, it would be disgusting. How would she feel knowing we had sex first?" I grimace, that thought scaring me. "You know she's liked you for a long time."

"She had a crush when she was a kid. She's grown up now."

"Her feelings didn't go away."

"If you knew that, why the fuck did you sleep with me?" I snap.

"Because I knew you'd never go near her. She's looking for love, and you're looking for a fuck. Hadley is amazing and she deserves to find a great guy. If you keep hanging around her, you'll give her the wrong idea and she'll get attached. Where does that leave her when you get bored?"

I shrug. "Maybe I won't get bored."

"Grim, you're not listening. Stay away from Hadley or I'll tell her everything."

"And she'll hate you for it."

"I'm her twin, she'll forgive me. All I'm saying is step away slowly and she'll get used to it. It's not like you're a thing. She can get over a crush."

HADLEY

It's been a whole day and I've heard nothing from Grim. Mav said he was on Meli watch earlier, but she came home hours ago and there's still no sign. I've texted and called to see if he's okay and I've gotten no response.

Grabbing my blanket and a book, I head downstairs. The bar is a hive of activity, so it will distract me. Arthur Taylor and his brothers are drinking with Mav, but I ignore them and tap him on the shoulder. "Have you heard from Grim?" I ask.

Mav shakes his head. "Do you want me to call him?"

"No. I'm sure he's just busy. Never mind."

Tommy Taylor, the youngest of the brothers, lifts the book in my hand and reads the title aloud. "The Concept of Law, huh?"

"She's a book queen," says Mav proudly.

"Clever too, the perfect package," says Arthur. "Tommy, go and tell Hadley about your case. She might be able to help."

I begin to shake my head, but Tommy hooks his arm in mine and leads me to another table. He goes into detail about a brawl he was recently involved in, but I'm distracted, constantly looking out the window for Grim. When I see his bike pull into the parking lot, I push down the urge to march out there and give him a piece of my mind for driving when he's already been temporarily banned. "So, what do you think?" asks Tommy, pulling me back into the room.

"Well, really, it's not up to me to say. Each solicitor has their own way of dealing with these things, and if you're not satisfied with your representative, I'm happy for you to contact my firm and book an appointment."

When I next look up, Grim is glaring down at me, and I suck in a breath. He looks hot as hell with a brooding expression. "You drove" is the first thing I mutter, and he nods. "Where did you go? I was worried."

His eyes flick to Tommy and he scoffs. "Looks like it," he says, then he stomps off towards the stairs. I frown in confusion, but it dawns on me he could have had a drink. I smile at Tommy and apologise. "Sorry, I have to . . ." I nod in the direction Grim went. "Call my office, I'd be happy to help." I head upstairs in time to see him stepping out of Meli's bedroom. "What are you doing?" I ask, and he looks up in surprise.

"What were you doing more like?" he snaps, marching past me and heading up the next flight of stairs to his room with me hot on his heels.

"Tommy was asking me for legal advice."

"Sure," he utters, sounding unconvinced.

"What's wrong with you? You went to get breakfast and then you disappeared."

"I don't need a nagging wife, Hadley," he drawls.

My mouth falls open. "I'm not nagging," I mutter. "I was worried."

"So, what were all the calls and the texts? Look, I'm tired," he says, sighing. "Can we do this tomorrow?"

"Do what? I don't know what we're doing." I almost yell.

Grim takes my arm and gently guides me towards the door. "Yah know, this is why I avoid this sort of thing. I hate having to answer to someone else. If I want to go off for the day, I can."

"I didn't say you couldn't... but you shouldn't be driving and—"

"Night." He closes the door in my face, and I stare at it for a few seconds, wondering if he's joking. When it's clear he isn't, I head back to my room, trying to work out what the hell just happened.

CHAPTER ELEVEN

GRIM

I lean back against my door and close my eyes. That will go down as one of the worst moments of my life, after watching my baby being aborted. I growl, balling my fists. What a fucking mess. How do I always fuck everything up? Mum appears in my mind, and I rip the bedroom door open and head for her room. She's the reason I'm like this!

I unlock Mum's door using the key hanging on the hook outside her room. She's on the bed, shaking and sweating, and the stale air smells so bad, I almost gag. "Get up!" I yell, and she jumps with fright. "Get up! I want you out of here."

She begins to slowly sit, but she's not fast enough for my liking, so I haul her up by her arm. She flinches, and it pisses me off more. "I'm not like them!" I yell, pulling her towards the door. "Years I had to watch you flinch like that, and you have the nerve to do it around me when I always protected you? Always!"

She stumbles. "Hudson, please—"

"This is what you wanted, wasn't it? To get out of here, so you can put more shit in your veins?"

"What's happened?" she whispers. "Why are you so mad?"

I drag her down the stairs, not caring that she's trying desperately to stay upright. "Because my life is a fucking mess and it's all your fault. You made me like this. Everything I touch turns to fucking shit, and it's your fault!"

Rylee rushes over and takes Mum's other arm. "Is everything okay?"

"Yes. Mum's leaving."

Rylee looks around frantically for someone else to back her up. "I don't think she's ready to leave, Grim."

"She'll be fine. She's spent years being fine."

"But the doctor is really pleased with her progress. And she's due her methadone shortly."

"She doesn't need it." I stop and pull out my wallet, taking out a bunch of bank notes and stuffing them into her hand. "There, that should cover it."

"Let me get Mav," begins Rylee, but I'm already opening the door.

Mum stands in the doorway, then she slowly turns to face me. "What happened today, Hudson?" she asks quietly. I clench my jaw when I recognise that flicker of kindness. I saw it only a handful of times when I was small, but it's been missing for a long time. "Someone's upset you," she continues, and she gently places a shaking hand on my cheek and smiles. "It's okay to be mad, I deserve it, but it won't make things better."

"Don't talk like you know me," I hiss. "You have no idea!"

I feel Mav's hand on my shoulder. "Wait in my office."

"No," I state, "I don't need to talk about this."

"I'm not asking, Grim. As your President, I'm telling you, go to my fucking office now."

Biting my lip, I shake my head and storm off in the direction of his office. I hate it when he pulls rank like that, and he knows it. He joins me five minutes later. "Carol is back in her room, safe, where she belongs." I glare at the floor. "Should we drink or hit the gym?" I ignore him. "You want me to choose? Good, cos I feel like beating your arse." Mav opens his gym bag and throws a set of boxing gloves my way. "Let's hit the basement, it's closer." The gloves land by my feet. "If you don't come willingly, I'll get some of the brothers to bring you. Then, I'll make them hold you while I get a few shots in."

I roll my eyes and grab the gloves. "You'll wish they held me back by the time I've finished with you," I declare, marching from the office and heading for the basement.

※

Boxing was how the men sorted things back in the days when Eagle was in charge. He loved a good fight, and it meant any dispute could be settled then and there. I never had to fight Mav, we hated all the bravado of the fight and usually avoided attending, but occasionally, Eagle would make sure we were there. These days, the only time we come down here is to spar.

Mav pulls out the pads, and I shake my head. "No way. You want to fight, get some gloves on."

"I don't want to fight. I want you to get some of that stress out and tell me what the fuck is going on in your head."

"You don't want to know." I go in the bag and pull another set of gloves. I shove them in his chest, and he sighs before starting to put them on.

"Are we going in full or sparring?"

I crack him on the jaw. It's unexpected and he stumbles back. "Fuck," he growls, wiping his bloodied lip on his arm.

"We're not sparring," I confirm.

He shrugs his shoulders a few times, loosening himself and, then he hits me back, busting my lip. He grins. "That's better."

We throw punches back and forth, occasionally causing minor damage. "Is it Hadley?" he eventually asks. I hit him harder, catching his cheek, but he shakes it off and smiles. "Did she get sick of your shit already?"

"No, she can't get enough of me, brother."

"Pres," he corrects. "So, it's about your mum?"

I double jab him in the stomach. "Nope."

"Bullshit." He hits the side of my head. "You were about to kick her out of here at two in the morning!"

"And you saved her arse yet again." I give him a few jabs in his side.

"You're pissed I'm helping her?" He laughs, then lays into me, backing me against the wall and landing punches over my body. He backs off, and I wince when pain shoots through my ribs. "I think I broke one," he says, smirking.

"She can't be helped. You don't listen."

"It's not your call, I'm in charge. Or is that your problem?"

I hit him in the face, busting his nose, and laugh. "Being President is going to your head, brother. I wouldn't want to be in your shoes for nothing."

"Yah know what I think?" he snaps, resting his hands on his knees and watching blood drip to the ground. "I think you don't know what the fuck is wrong. I think you need to see someone for depression."

"I'm not depressed," I growl out.

"You are, Grim. I've seen it before, remember. I was right then, and I'm right now."

"You don't know what the fuck is going on in my life right now, brother. You're too busy rescuing people to see what's going on."

"Then tell me!" he yells.

I rip the gloves from my hands and throw them to the ground. "We're done here," I state and head for the steps.

"Tell me what to do and I'll do it, Grim. Whatever it takes to help you." I ignore him, leaving him dripping with blood, and make my way upstairs.

I pace outside Hadley's room, stopping several times and place my hand on the door handle but pull away before I go in. Do I tell her everything and hope she likes me enough to forgive me? I'm scared to risk it. She might never speak to me again, and I hate that thought.

The door suddenly opens, and I spin to see Hadley wearing my shirt. We stare at each other silently for a few seconds before she turns back towards her bed, leaving the door open for me to follow. She gets into bed, throws me a pillow and sheet, then turns the lamp off and lays down. I stare at the bedding in my arms before sighing and dropping it to the ground beside her bed. I kick off my boots and sit on the floor. "I fucked up."

"Yeah, you did," she whispers.

"I want to tell you," I mutter, "but I'm scared." I sound like a pussy, but with Hadley, I don't mind cos I know she won't judge me. I can let my guard down.

"I'm mad at you," she says firmly. "Don't make me feel bad about that."

I smile, even though she can't see me. "I'm not trying to. You're right to be mad."

"What happened to your face?"

"Your brother got his arse kicked."

"Looks like you didn't come off lightly either."

"I realised something today." She remains quiet, so I continue. "I can't function when you're not around me. I'm so used to running to you with problems that when that option is taken away, I don't know what to do."

"Did you sort the problem?"

My heart squeezes at the image of Meli's face as they sucked my baby from her and angry tears fill my eyes. Men don't fucking cry. I can hear Eagle's words ringing in my ears and I swipe the tears away quickly. "Yeah," I whisper.

"Go to sleep, Grim. Tomorrow is a new day."

I lie down on the floor and pull the sheet over me. I stare at the ceiling, wondering if Meli is okay or if it's haunting her too.

HADLEY

"Hads, your sister isn't feeling well, could you take her some breakfast?" Mum asks, and I nod, grabbing a plate and filling it.

"What's wrong with her?" I ask.

"You know Meli," she says, winking. "Dramatic. It's probably period pains."

I laugh and head up to her room. She's lying in bed and her eyes are red from crying. I place the plate on the bedside table and sit beside her, stroking her hair from her face. "What's wrong?"

"I'm being silly," she mumbles, her voice croaky from crying. "It's just a bit of a stomach ache."

I smile, remembering Mum's comment. I pull the covers back. "Well, how about we watch a film and—" I stare wide-eyed at her pyjamas. "Jesus Christ, Meli! What the fuck?" She looks down too and pales. There's so much blood, it looks like a murder scene. "That's not a period, is it?"

Meli begins to hyperventilate and cry all at the same time. Taking her hand, I crouch so I'm eye-level. "Okay, it's fine. Just breathe. Nice and slow, in through the nose, out through the mouth." She copies me, but her eyes are wide with panic and I can tell she's scared. "Maybe it's just a really bad period, but I'm gonna get Mum to come and check. Stay calm."

I run downstairs and whisper to Mum that I need her urgently. Grim catches my eye, but I don't have time to explain as I pull her out the kitchen.

Mum lifts the covers back and raises her eyebrows in shock. "Okay, my darling girl. I'm sure it's nothing, but we should get you checked out. I'm going to call an ambulance."

Meli panics more, shaking her head. "No. No. I don't need a hospital."

"Sweetheart, it's better to be safe than—"

"I was pregnant. I lo—" She lets out a shaky breath. "I lost it. This is normal."

My mouth falls open. "Pregnant?"

"Yes. Long story really, but it's fine now. Well . . . apart from this. See if Doc's around."

Mum pushes me to the door. "Find Doc."

I stumble from the room straight into Grim's chest. He steadies me, looking worried. "Are you okay?"

"Can you go and find Doc?"

"What's wrong?" he asks. "Has something happened to Meli?"

"She's had a miscarriage."

Grim frowns. "What?"

"She never told me she was pregnant," I whisper. "Why wouldn't she tell me that?"

"I'll go and find Doc," Grim mutters, heading downstairs. I slide down the hall wall. We share everything, though I know we've had some secrets. Meli being abused by Ripper was a huge shock to us all, not just me. And I've been seeing Grim without her knowledge, but it's only because I don't want to hear her negativity. But pregnant? I didn't even know she was seeing anyone.

We all wait outside while Doc is in with Meli. Mum stares at the ground, and Grim paces. I can't help but think he's upset because it's another thing he didn't see, just like when he missed Ripper. Mum decides to make us each a cup of tea and disappears. "Do you still like her?" I blurt out. Grim stops pacing to stare at me. "I know you used to—"

"No, Hadley, I don't. How can you ask me that?"

"It's just hard to turn off feelings."

"What do you take me for? You think I'd fuck you but love your twin?"

I feel the blush creep up my cheeks. I don't want us to fight anymore. I don't even know why I asked cos now's not the time to make shit about me just because I feel insecure. Grim holds out his hand, and I take it so he can pull me to my feet. He pushes me against the wall, caging me in with a hand at either side of my head. "It's you, Hads. It's always gonna be you, no matter what." And then, he kisses me. He pours everything into that kiss, taking my breath away, and when he pulls back, I smile. That's all I needed to know.

∞

I crawl up Grim's body and lay my head against his chest. We're both out of breath from another lovemaking session, our second today. Meli wanted to be left alone, and I guess she's avoiding questions that Mum and I both have. Grim draws lazy circles on my back. "I was thinking," he murmurs, placing a kiss on my head. "We should continue to keep this between us for now. Meli's going through enough, and if you're right and she really does hate me, she won't want to deal with the news of us right now."

"Yeah, I was thinking the same. I don't want to ram my happiness down her throat when she's so fragile."

"Who'd ya think the father is?"

I scoff. "Who knows. She's been keeping so much from me lately, I don't feel like I know her at all."

"Maybe he wasn't important."

"Maybe he was an arse who got my sister pregnant and left her alone to deal with it."

"Do you think she knows who he is? She's been going out a lot lately with Rosey, and who knows what they get up to."

I shrug. "Maybe. Maybe not. I'm sure she'll tell me when she's ready. And when I find out, I'm gonna kill him."

Grim tips my head back to look at him. "You're too nice for that."

"No one messes with my twin and gets away with it," I say, grinning. He kisses me on the nose and wraps me in his arms.

CHAPTER TWELVE

GRIM

"How the hell do we end up doing Arthur's shit?" I hiss in Mav's ear. We're crammed in the back of a van on the way to one of Nick Cambridge's casinos.

"It's a good money-maker."

"What happened to getting clean, Mav?"

"Pres," he corrects me, "and it's a little late raising your concerns now when all the plans are set. Maybe if you'd have turned up to church last week when we first discussed this, I'd have listened."

"I had shit to do."

"Always your excuse. It pisses me the fuck off you're doubting me. Have I made a bad decision yet?"

"Yes," Ghost chips in. "You made him VP."

Everyone chuckles, and I stick my middle finger up at him. "It's easy money, in and out. The security guard will let us in the side door, the cameras are going down at midnight, and we'll have three minutes to grab the cash and run," Mav explains again.

And that's exactly what we do. We fill our bags with bundles of cash and walk out the back door like nothing happened. Nick Cambridge's problem is he doesn't expect anyone to mess with him. He certainly isn't expecting three of his biggest casinos to be hit at exactly the same time. Arthur is leading the other hits, and provided they went well, we're all a little richer this evening.

We all meet back at the clubhouse as planned. Arthur chucks some bags in the centre of the table, and Mav adds ours. Arthur holds up his mobile as it rings and he smiles smugly before saying, "Right on time." He answers, putting the call on speaker for us all to hear. "Mr. Cambridge, what can I do for you?"

"Arthur, I've been done over!" yells Nick Cambridge.

"That's unfortunate."

"Unfortunate? It's a lot more that fucking unfortunate! I want my money found."

"I know where your money is, Nick. Calm the fuck down." I glance at Mav, confused. "Before I return it to you, we'll need to talk."

"You've got it?"

"You need to call off the hit on the VP from The Perished Riders."

"No way! He put me in hospital and took my wife and child!"

"Talking of which, you'll need to let that divorce of yours go through smoothly."

"What's this?"

"I'll let you think over those terms and get back to me. Don't take too long, I'm not a patient man."

"Bu—"

"Good. Speak soon." Arthur disconnects the call and places the mobile back in his pocket. "Let's hope he comes to his senses."

"What's to stop him calling the police?" asks Ghost.

"Nothing really, but I've gotten to know him pretty well and he's not one to snitch. If he was, your VP would be in prison already."

"So, all this was about helping the club?" I ask.

"It's about helping you, brother. Which, again, you'd know if you attended church when we were making plans. I can't have you walking around with a target on your back. It puts Hadley in danger." Mav smirks, and I feel the other brothers looking at me for an explanation.

"It was supposed to stay a secret for a little longer," I mutter, and the room erupts into cheers.

"About fucking time," says Copper, smacking me on the back. "Your dad would be over the moon."

"I think he'd be as surprised as me," I point out, and he laughs. "Guys, I'm serious, this isn't common knowledge, and Hadley doesn't want anyone to know just yet, so keep quiet for a bit longer."

∞

After church, I head up to Meli's room. I tap lightly on the door and step in. She's watching television, but she pauses it and glares at me. "What?"

"I just wanted to see how you're doing."

"Fine."

I close the door and take a seat. "Amelia, stop being such a bitch. I'm checking in to see how you're doing and to say I've been worried."

She sighs. "Sorry. I'm tired and I don't know how I feel. Messed up mainly."

"Yeah, I can't get it out of my head either. If it was the right thing to do, why does it feel like shit?"

She shrugs. "It'll get easier. Just give it time, I guess."

"Do you regret it?"

For a second, I think she might cry, but eventually, she shakes her head. "No."

"Your brother's been trying to set me up with Hadley," I say, changing the subject. I want to try and change her mind on the whole thing, and I think if she knows Maverick is on side, she'll eventually come around to the idea.

"Why would he do that?"

I shrug. "He thinks she'll be good for me."

"But he doesn't know we had sex. If he knew, he wouldn't say that."

I shift uncomfortably. "It wasn't a relationship, Meli. We had sex a couple of times."

"And I got pregnant. If you're trying to tell me something, I suggest you just say it."

"It's just . . . I've been spending a lot of time with her, and she's alright, yah know."

Tears fill her eyes. "How dare you sit at my bedside after everything I've been through and try to ask if I'll accept you and Hadley."

"It's not like you want to be with me!" I snap.

"So you decide to go for her? How will she feel knowing she's second best?"

"She's not. That's not what I meant," I argue.

"It's what it looks like, Grim. She deserves better. Stay away from her."

"I don't know if I can," I mutter.

She scoffs angrily. "Fine. Go for it. But you have to tell her everything first."

"Why?" I snap. "Why can't we just forget it ever happened and move on? That's what you said at the hospital, that we could forget it all and move forward!"

"I didn't know you'd be moving on to my fucking twin sister!" she hisses. "She deserves to know, so she can make up her own mind. You know it's wrong, that's why you don't want me to tell her, because she'll never be with you after this, and we both know it."

I stand angrily. "This was a waste of time."

HADLEY

I'm in the shower when I hear Grim come into my room. Minutes later, he's tugging me from the shower and wrapping me in his arms. "I'm getting you wet," I point out, laughing.

"I don't care," he mumbles into my neck. He drops to his knees and runs his fingers through my pussy. I shiver against his touch and grip his shoulders. "I missed you."

"Where were you all night?"

"Playing robbers with your brother."

"He's a bad influence," I joke.

Grim inserts his fingers into me, and I gasp. "We need to spend the day in here, locked away from the world."

"Nice idea, Burglar Bill, but I have things to do."

"It's Sunday. Who works on a Sunday?"

"A woman after a promotion."

He shakes his head. "No, not today. Today, we're hiding here." He buries his head between my legs, licking along my opening. I push my fingers into his hair, closing my eyes as he works his magic. When I'm close to coming, he stands, and I groan in protest. "Stay."

"Grim, I have to go to work. What's wrong?"

He sweeps me up in his arms and carries me through to the bed. "I just need to be with you today."

"I know we're keeping this quiet, but people will get suspicious if we're both missing all day again. We spend every spare moment in here."

He bends me over and runs his hands over my bare arse. "Do you know how hot you look like that?"

"Stop changing the subject."

I hear his belt unfasten and glance over my shoulder. He grabs a handful of my hair and tips my head back. I feel his erection pushing at my opening. "I'm tired of talking," he murmurs. He moves fast, fucking hard and taking me by surprise. He slams into me over and over, keeping hold of my hair. He suddenly stops and turns me around, pushing me to my knees and gripping his cock in his hand. I automatically take him in my mouth, and he closes his eyes in pleasure as I suck him. I know the moment he's about to come because his panting is out of control and his cock tightens. I let him fall from my mouth, and his eyes shoot open. I smile up at him. He stopped just as I was about to come, so there's no way he's having all the pleasure. He grins and pulls me to stand. "You think you're clever," he says.

I scream in surprise when he picks me up, and I wrap my legs around his waist. He pushes into me and nuzzles my neck, fucking me like I weigh nothing. We come together and collapse on the bed, still wrapped around each other.

After a few minutes rest, he runs kisses down my neck and over my breasts. "I have to go," I argue, trying to push him away. He sucks a nipple into his mouth, and I arch my back. He has way too much power over my body. "Grim, please," I whisper, but it's a mix of begging him to keep going and to let me go. "Don't you ever get tired?"

"Not when it comes to you. We should get our own place," he adds.

I laugh, confused by his odd behaviour. "But we live here."

"Just imagine what it would be like to have our own place. I'd get you to myself all day and night," he mutters, growling as he enters me again. "We could walk around naked."

"You're acting weird."

"I'm not. I'm seeing clearly for fucking once and I don't want to let you go."

"You don't have to." I laugh, unsure why he's saying all this. "We can tell everyone once Meli's feeling better."

"That's when things get messy, though. Everyone will be involved."

"Nobody bothers Rylee or Gracie. Stop overthinking."

He speeds up again, slamming into me until it's almost uncomfortable. "Grim," I mutter, pushing against his shoulder. He grunts, his rhythm fast and jerky. "Grim," I repeat. It's like he's lost in a memory and that freaks me out more, so I hit his shoulder hard, once, twice, a third time, and eventually, he blinks and looks down at me. "Stop," I snap. "Stop!"

He immediately stops. "Shit, sorry. Fuck. I was . . ."

I push him from me. "You weren't here, I get it."

"I . . . Hadley, I—"

"Forget it. The worst thing is, I'm starting to get used to this weird behaviour." I sigh heavily, then head back to the bathroom to shower for a second time. Grim follows me, leaning against the sink unit with his arms folded over his chest and his head bowed.

"I'm sorry," he whispers.

"It's fine."

"It's not fine. I'm really sorry, Hads. I'm scared."

"Of what?" I snap, frustrated with this same bullshit.

"Of losing you," he shouts.

I stare at him, my heart breaking. He looks so vulnerable and worried. "Grim, you won't lose me. Why would you? Do you know how long I've waited for this? For us?"

He glances at me, and his eyes are so full of pain, it almost breaks me. I step from the shower and wrap myself in a towel. Standing before him, I run a hand over his cheek. "I'm not going anywhere."

"Promise?" he asks, and I nod. "Because I can't stand the thought of you walking out on me too."

I wrap my arms around his neck and hold him. I feel his shoulders shaking and realise he's crying. I don't think I've ever seen any of the men here cry. The fact he's doing it in front of me shows he trusts me enough to let me see that side of him, and it means the world. I hold him tighter. "No matter what, right?" he mumbles, and I nod again. "Words, Hads. I need to hear it."

"No matter what, Grim. I won't leave you, no matter what."

"I want us to have a place away from here."

"Why?"

"I just . . . I'd feel better having our own space. Away from the drama."

"But this is your home. With your brothers. Just sleep on it, Grim. You're tired, and you've been gone all night." It's the only explanation I have for his desperate plea of reassurance.

He nods. "Stay."

I bite my lower lip. I've been so distracted lately, I'm behind at work. "I guess I could work from home today." He smiles with relief, and I follow him back to the bed, where he lies down. I settle beside him and open my laptop. I make a decision to speak to Mav about Grim, he knows him better than anyone and might know what's really going on. Maybe a place of our own wouldn't be so bad, but I'd miss being here with all the noise and craziness.

"It's early days, Hads, but I think I'm falling for you," he mumbles sleepily.

I gently run my fingers through his hair, and he closes his eyes. "Same," I whisper.

Later, I leave Grim sleeping and head downstairs to find Mav. He's in his office looking just as exhausted as Grim did earlier. I go in and shut the door, taking a seat. "Come in," he mutters sarcastically. "Make yourself comfortable."

"I'm worried about Grim," I state, and he drops his pen down and looks at me.

"That makes two of us."

"He was acting crazy today. Did something happen last night?"

Mav shakes his head. "No. He's been off for days. Last night, Arthur severed ties with a man he's been trying to get on side for weeks. He did that for this club, to help Grim because I thought the stress of having Cambridge put a target on his back was getting to him." He pinches the bridge of his nose. "But he didn't seem any less stressed when I told him. And all the business with his mum isn't helping."

"He wants us to get a place together." Mav doesn't bother to hide his shocked expression. "I know," I mutter, smirking. "Imagine, an actual man who wants to live with me."

"It's not that, Hads. Grim loves being around the guys. I know he gets itchy feet sometimes and talks about hitting the road, but he'd always come back for the brothers. Living away from us? It's not like him."

"Maybe," I grin, "he's fallen madly in love with me, and I've changed him."

"Or maybe he's worrying about something? Something we don't know about. He wants to run. He's been telling me as much for the last few months." Mav falls silent, trying hard to work out what Grim would be running from.

"Do you think he's worried about the brothers finding out about us?"

Mav shakes his head. "No. They already know."

"What?"

"I accidentally let it slip last night."

"He never said."

"Why the secret anyway?"

I shrug. "We just liked our little bubble. Then Meli happened, so we decided to wait."

"Well, Meli is feeling much better today. I'm sure she'll be up and about later. There's no reason to keep it hidden. Let's get it out there and celebrate, see if that helps him relax."

I nod in agreement. "I think I'll tell her first. She's not his biggest fan, and I'm sure she'll have plenty to say."

"Maybe while you're there, you can ask her who the fuck got her pregnant," Mav suggests, looking pissed. "I can't kill a shadow." I nod, just as curious to know.

CHAPTER THIRTEEN

HADLEY

Meli smiles, pleased to see me when I go into her room. "You look much better," I tell her, taking a seat.

"I'm bored out of my mind. Mum won't let me move from the bed, and she's driving me insane."

"You gave us a fright yesterday," I remind her. "Meli, why didn't you tell me?"

"I don't know," she admits. "I only found out two weeks ago, and you were busy with work. I just didn't want to bother you."

I don't correct her. I was too busy with Grim hiding in my room, and I feel guilty as hell. "And the father?"

"A one-night stand," she mutters, and my eyes widen. "I know, okay, I'm not proud of it."

"You have to stop this destructive behaviour, Meli. Since Rosey came back, you've been worse."

"Don't blame Rosey. I'm an adult. She's fun to be around and she's there for me."

I narrow my eyes, and she looks guilty all of a sudden. "You told her?"

Meli shrugs. "She was around."

"You told Rosey and not me!"

"Let's not fight," she mutters. "We're always fighting."

"Is it any wonder? What did I do wrong? She knew about Ripper, and now, she knows this, so what other secrets do you run to her with?"

"It's not like that. She's my friend."

"We're twins, we're supposed to share everything." As the words fall from my mouth, Grim and our own little secret comes to mind, and I press my lips together in a tight line. I stand. "Seeing as we're full of secrets lately, I'll tell you mine. I'm in a relationship."

Meli sits up straighter, smiling. "Wow. Hads, that's great." Then her smile fades. "With who?" she asks, suspiciously. I hesitate and she takes a deep, calming breath. "Tell me it's not Grim."

"We like each other. It's early days and we're taking it slow, but we're adults. And it's nothing to do with you, so I'd appreciate if you kept your negative thoughts to yourself."

She surprises me by bursting into tears. I stare for a second before reacting, rushing over and wrapping my arms around her. "Are you okay?"

"I'm shocked," she says between sniffles. "Grim?"

I smile, tucking her hair behind her ear. "I know you hate him, but you've always known how I feel about him, and finally, he sees me! I've waited so long for that."

She gives me a sad smile. "I miss us spending time together. I'm sorry I didn't tell you."

I kiss her cheek. "I'm sorry I haven't been around much. I'll make more of an effort."

GRIM

Something wet splashes over my face and I sit up in shock, gasping for breath while wiping the ice water from my eyes. "Fuck!"

"You and fucking Hadley," hisses Meli before she proceeds to pound her fists against my chest.

I grab her wrists. "Meli, stop! Stop!"

"How could you?"

"I tried to tell you. It just happened. I couldn't stop my feelings for her."

"Bullshit! Fucking bullshit, Grim! You're in her bed. In her fucking bed!" She grips her head like she can't process any of it. "You better tell her."

"I can't do that."

"You don't have a choice!" she screams, and I dive up from the bed in panic. I lock the door and turn to her.

"Meli, she's happy. I can't crush her like that. None of this was supposed to happen, but it has, and I can't risk everything for something that was a one-off."

"It was not a one-off, and I got pregnant!"

"But you're not now, are you, so it's over and done with. Why would I bring it up with Hadley when she's so happy?"

"We've been over this so many times. You have to be honest because if this comes out later, she'll hate us even more."

"We're not telling her, Amelia. I can't lose her, I'm sorry."

"So, you really like her?" she asks, and I nod. "I hate you for putting me in this situation."

"Trust me, I hate myself right now. If I could take it back, I would."

"This can't ever get out, Grim. If this is the decision, then we stick to it no matter what."

I nod eagerly, hardly daring to believe she's agreeing to this. "Thank you."

"I'm not doing this for you. It's for her. I know how much she likes you. Don't fucking hurt her, Grim, or I'll get Rosey to kill you."

I smile. "Promise."

It's like a weight is lifted. I shower and dress and change Hadley's wet sheets. When I go to find her, as usual, she's under the oak tree. "Let's go out for dinner."

She looks up. "You want to take me for dinner?"

I laugh, taking her hands and pulling her to stand. "Yes. I want us to eat dinner in a nice place like normal couples. But you'll have to drive."

∞

We find a restaurant that lets us in with no problems, mainly because I've removed my kutte for the evening. Usually, owners of places like this can be uptight about who they let in. We get a window seat and are handed our menus.

"Good sleep?" Hadley asks.

The waitress puts a jug of water on the table. "Yeah. I missed waking up next to you, though."

"Some of us can't lie around in bed all day," she jokes. "Tomorrow, I have to go to work. No distracting me."

"Scout's honour," I promise.

"I spoke with Mav today," she says, avoiding eye contact, which immediately makes me suspicious. "He's worried about you."

"There's no need to be. I'm fine."

"I'm worried too."

I pour us each a glass of water, trying to remain calm. "Like I said, I'm all good."

"He thinks you're running from something." I grind my teeth to avoid snapping at her. "But I think you might have something medically wrong." When I stare at her blankly, she continues. "I was looking up mental health and bi-polar came up. Have you heard of it?"

"I'm not bi-polar, Hadley."

"It's quite common and nothing to be ashamed of."

"I'm not bi-polar."

"The erratic behaviour, the highs and lows—"

"Hadley," I snap, and she stops talking. I glance around to make sure no one is looking at us. "There's nothing wrong. I was worried about something, but I'm not now. I've sorted it, so I'm fine."

"Worried about what?"

"It's not important now. What's important is we're happy, we're together, and I want the world to know. So, let's enjoy dinner, go and have a drink, and be a normal couple."

She smiles, relaxing back in her chair. "Okay."

"Okay."

We're tucking into our food when she leans closer and says accusingly, "You told the guys about us."

"How do you know that?"

"Mav told me."

"Then he would have also said it was him who told the brothers and not me."

She grins. "What did they say?"

"They were happy for us. But you seem a lot calmer than I thought you'd be. Didn't you want to keep it quiet because of Meli?"

At the mention of her sister's name, she almost chokes on her food and takes a mouthful of water. "About that . . . I told her already."

"Really?" I ask, acting surprised. "What did she say?"

"She was fine . . . in the end."

"Good, because we're together no matter what and no one is coming between us."

HADLEY

I feel happier. Grim seems to be like his old self again and it's a relief to see. He makes jokes and fools around. Stopping every few steps to kiss me. He grips my hand like it's a lifeline, and I want to pinch myself to check it's not a dream. I never thought the day would come when Grim would like me back, and not only like me, but act like he's obsessed. He can't stop touching me, and when I go to the bathroom in the bar, he waits right outside.

I'm washing my hands when he steps in and locks the door. "What are you doing?" I ask, laughing as he wraps his arms around me.

"Wanna try something?"

"Depends."

"Take off your underwear."

"No! What if my skirt rides up?"

"That's part of the excitement." I can't resist the cheeky smile he gives me, so I allow him to reach under my skirt and remove my knickers. He sticks them in his pocket and takes me by the hand, unlocks the door, and leads me back to the booth we'd already claimed.

We have a couple more drinks as he tells me tales of when he and Mav were kids and the stuff they got up to. "Do you want kids?" I ask, and his smile falters slightly.

"I don't know. It's not something I've ever thought I wanted, but since you . . ." He leaves the sentence open, and I can't hide my grin. He laughs and pulls me in for a kiss. I feel his hand slide up my thigh and gasp when his finger brushes my opening. "Don't give the game away, Hads," he whispers against my lips. As he rubs circles over my clit, I bite my lip, concentrating on keeping my face neutral. The booth is pretty dark, the music is pumping, and everyone around us is shouting to be heard, so I doubt anyone is paying attention to us. He suddenly lifts me, sitting me on his lap. "Lift slightly," he instructs and unfastens his trousers. "Now, sit down real slow."

He holds his erection at my entrance, and I slowly slide down, gripping the table edge for support. "Good girl," he whispers, moving my hair to one side and nibbling my neck. I feel full and turned on, and we're not even moving. His hand moves under my skirt and goes back to rubbing me. Occasionally, I twitch or fidget and I hear his groan. "Lean forward, rest your elbow on the table." I do as he says, lifting off him slightly, which gives him the space to slowly move. If anyone were to watch us closely, it would be obvious, but looking around, everyone is still minding their own business.

I feel the warmth of my pending orgasm and move my hands to his knees. He pulls me to sit back on him and grabs my hips, slightly rocking me back and forth. We're hardly moving at all, but it doesn't stop the mind-blowing orgasm ripping through me. I jerk, unable to control it, and hear him gasping as he reaches his own orgasm.

"We gotta get home, baby. I need more of that," he whispers in my ear. Grabbing some napkins from the table, he discreetly wipes me as I stand, dumping them in the trash as we leave.

CHAPTER FOURTEEN

GRIM

"Slight problem," announces Mav in church the next day. "Cambridge isn't playing ball. He sent some thugs to smash up one of Arthur's bars last night."

"Fuck, so all we did was piss him off?" asks Ghost.

"On the plus side, we're rich," I say, smirking.

"Great, we can bail your arse out of prison," Ghost replies sarcastically.

"Arthur said to be patient. He thinks Nick's just throwing his toys out the pram. Once he's had his tantrum, he'll do as we ask."

"How will we know he's taken the target off my back?" I ask.

"You'll still be around to annoy us," says Copper, and I grin. It feels good to be relaxed and stress-free.

"Arthur's got feelers out everywhere, so he'll know who Cambridge has asked."

"So, why can't Arthur just order them not to carry it out? This is his area too, right?" asks Ghost.

"Depends on what Cambridge is willing to pay, for a start," I say. "He'll always find one scumbag who will do anything for cash. I gotta go make peace with him."

"Make peace?" asks Mav, laughing. "What the fuck did you have on your cereal today, rays of happiness?"

"I got myself into this mess, I'll get out of it. He's a businessman. I'll offer to do some dirty work for him."

"It's too risky. Besides, that won't save his wife, and we can't partner up with a dick like him. Women will lose faith in the club."

"Then what do we do? Because I don't wanna die, and Harriett ain't going back home to him," I say.

"We'll be patient a little while longer. If he doesn't see sense, we'll come up with a plan. Maybe this time we could blow his fucking casino up!"

After church, I head up to Mum's room. The door is open, but she isn't there and the sheets are changed. The windows are wide and a moment of panic hits me hard. I run downstairs and into the kitchen but stop in my tracks. Mum is at the table, drinking tea with Mama B and Hadley. They all turn to me, and Hadley smiles. "She's feeling a little better."

"I thought she'd . . . never mind."

"Come join us," says Mama B, holding out her hand. I take it and sit beside her. "Why don't we leave you two to talk?" she suggests. Hadley nods, and they make a quick exit.

"Smooth," I mutter, and Mum smiles. She looks pale and tired still and way too thin, but she isn't shaking or sweating. "How are you really feeling?"

"Good . . . ish. It's hard, but today feels like a better day."

"You look a little better."

"Don't lie. I look like shit." We both laugh. "Brea was telling me about Eagle." I nod. "I didn't see that coming."

"Neither did we."

"And his other kid is here, at the club?" I nod again. "Seems like Mav is making good changes. The club was never so forgiving before."

"He's trying. Now the dead wood is gone, it's easier."

"I have so much explaining to do," she says quietly.

"Stick around this time, then you can explain all you want." She nods. "This is it, Ma. After this chance, there'll never be another from me. If you fuck this up, I'm cutting you off."

"I don't blame you," she whispers. "You deserved better. And so did Xzavier." I wait patiently for her to continue. "He's sixteen now. I don't know where he is because his dad took him from me when he was less than a month old. But you deserve to know about him."

"Jesus, you had another kid?"

She nods. "Your dad knew. He chose not to tell you because he didn't want to upset you. I was doing a great job of that all by myself. But hopefully, now I'm getting straight, I can put a lot of past mistakes right."

She takes my hand, and I stare at her bony fingers. I guess I knew deep down there was always a possibility she'd have other kids, but I don't know how I feel about having a brother. A real blood brother who lost his mum just like I did.

While Hadley is using Mav's office to work, I sit on the worn couch and sip a whiskey. "You went to work all day, and you come home and work some more."

"There's a promotion coming up and I want it," she mutters, staring hard at the laptop.

"Why? You don't need to work—I've got you."

She grins. "I want to work. Who would help you out of driving bans?"

I laugh. "You said yourself, it'll be a hefty fine and a ban. It's stupid I even have to go to court."

"Grim, you had six points on your licence already. They had no choice but to report you for the offence."

I make my way over to her and kiss her on the head. "You sound like a lawyer."

"Good. Now go, so I can work."

"If you're gonna be my ol' lady, you'll have to chauffeur me around until I get my licence back. You won't have time to work."

"You have more than enough brothers around this place to help you out. I'm not quitting, so forget it."

"What if we have kids?"

She looks up. "You hate kids."

"If it keeps you here beside me, I'm gonna fill you with 'em."

She rolls her eyes, shaking her head. "That reminds me, I'd better get the shot again."

"Yeah, you'd better," I whisper, kissing her again. "I ain't ready to share you just yet." It was on the tip of my tongue to mention my brother, but I didn't. Instead, I let her work and join my brothers in the bar, the brothers I grew up with and know better than anyone. Maybe I don't need to know Xzavier after all.

HADLEY

The nurse clicks away on her laptop. It was a week before I could get an appointment to get my contraceptive shot, and the fact I've had to nip out of work is stressing me out. I have to meet Grim at the courthouse for his telling off from the judge in exactly an hour. "Ms. Maverick, your shot ran out six weeks ago."

I glare at her impatiently. "No, I was due at the end of this month."

She shakes her head. "No. It was an eight-week shot."

Dread fills me. "No, no, no, no. Why would I have the eight-week one? It's always twelve weeks. I always take the twelve weeks."

She looks back at her computer screen. "It says here you had some concerns about side effects last time you were here."

My conversation with the last nurse hits me, and I wince. "Oh god."

"And you agreed to have the shorter one to give you time to think about other options?"

I cover my mouth. "Yes, I remember."

"Have you been using contraception?"

I shake my head. "No, I thought I was covered."

"Before I can give it to you again, we'll need to test."

I check my watch. "I have to be back at work. Does it take long?"

She shakes her head and hands me a pot. "Not if you can pee now."

∞

"Sorry," I puff, rushing up the court steps towards Grim and Mav, "I got held up."

"Everything okay?" asks Grim, and I nod, forcing a smile.

Heading inside, we're called straight before the judge, who happens to be Harry. I see in Grim's face he's pissed. He orders Grim to stand, which only aggravates him more, but I kick his ankle and give him a look that tells him to behave. This is normal court etiquette.

He stands, patiently listening while the judge berates him for his stupidity and lack of concern for the safety of other road users and pedestrians. He orders him to pay the court costs, a five hundred pound fine, and bans him from driving for two years.

I thank the judge as Grim storms out with Mav hot on his heels. I find them outside. "Two years!" repeats Grim in disbelief.

"It's standard in most drunk driving cases."

"It's because he fucking likes you," he snaps, "and I'm a biker. He was discriminating."

"No, Grim. You were caught drunk driving. He was right—you could have killed someone, so you deserve the punishment. Take it like a man," I snap, marching off.

He catches up to me and takes me by the arm. "What's wrong?" I can't tell him I'm fine because when he spins me to face him, tears are already filling my eyes. "Hads, I'm sorry. I didn't mean to get mad," he says, pulling me into his arms. "Thanks for being there today."

"I'm pregnant," I blurt out against his chest. I know he's heard me because I feel him tense. "Around four weeks." I give him a second to process. "Say something."

"I thought you were on contraception," he mutters.

"Not that. Don't say that." I pull away. "Tell me you're happy or angry or something, but don't do the whole blame thing."

"It's hard not to, Hadley, when you told me you were sorted!"

"I missed my shot. It was an accident."

"An accident is missing your dentist appointment or forgetting to buy bread." I frown at his weird analogy. "It's not missing your shot, the one thing stopping you getting pregnant and ruining what we have!"

"We could stand here and argue about this all day, but it doesn't change anything. I last got the shot when I wasn't having sex, and she changed it to an eight-week plan. I usually have twelve, so I forgot. I fucked up, I'm sorry, but I'm still pregnant and it still involves you."

He stares at the ground with his hands on his hips, and I see the devastation on his face. He isn't ready, I know he isn't, and we're so early in this relationship that the timing is completely wrong, but keeping it from him didn't seem right either. And deep down, as scared as I am, I keep thinking that we made a baby and I can't help but feel a small spark of love for the tiny little bean.

GRIM

She's watching me, waiting for me to say it's all going to be fine, but it isn't. When Meli finds out about this, she'll throw a fit. And I can't blame her. This wasn't part of my dream when I decided to be with Hadley. Kids? The thought makes me shudder. I glance back to check Mav hasn't heard, but he's talking into his mobile and walking down the courthouse steps in the direction of his bike. "We should go back to the club," I mutter.

"That's it? That's all you've got?" she exclaims in disbelief.

"What the fuck do you want me to say?" I snap, causing her to take a step back, and I feel like a prick. "I just need a minute to process," I add more calmly.

We get back to the club and Hadley goes straight to her room. I want to follow, my whole body pulls in her direction, but I can't because my head isn't in the right place, and I don't want to be the reason she cries again.

I sit at the bar and ask Nelly for my usual, which she hands me with a smile. "You look like someone just stole your ice cream."

"Bad day," I mutter, draining the glass and holding it out for a refill.

"We all have those. Just remember there's always someone worse off than you."

"You reckon? Like who?"

Nelly shrugs. "Think about all the people who would have lost someone today or the people given terrible news like cancer prognosis and shit. Someone's life ended today, but the world just keeps turning like it doesn't matter."

"That's uplifting, thanks for the TED talk," I joke, half laughing, then I sigh. "It's hard to think about stuff like that when you feel shit though. I know people have it worse than me, but I'm still fucked off. Do you want kids, Nelly?"

She thinks for a minute. "I used to, but then I see what the world has become and I think it's cruel."

I laugh. "You are just a bundle of happiness today."

"Sorry, I guess I'm having a bad day too. Look, whatever's bothering you is not gonna get solved if you sit here drinking all night. I see far too many of you guys doing it. Go face the problem."

I sigh, standing. "Fine, but if it all goes wrong, I'm blaming you."

I find Hadley tapping away on her laptop. She ignores me when I enter the room, and continues to do so as I take off my boots and head for the shower. She's still busy working when I return wrapped in a towel. "We're like a married couple already," I say, "ignoring each other because of an argument."

"I'm not ignoring you—I'm busy."

I kneel beside her on the bed and take the laptop away. She rolls her eyes. "You're ignoring me." I put my finger under her chin and tip her head back, forcing her to look at me. "I used to laugh at Mav when he'd be moody because Rylee wasn't talking to him. I didn't get the fuss. I used to tell him not to stress over it and to have a night out with the boys, but he wouldn't. He'd sneak off to find her and beg her to forgive him, and I'd call him a pussy. But I get it now. I don't like it. I don't like that you're mad at me, and I hate that I've upset you."

"I'm not upset," she whispers, her eyes watering. "I'm disappointed."

I groan and fall beside her, holding a hand over my heart. "Oh god, that's so much worse," I say, and she laughs a little.

"I needed you today, and you were a dick."

I roll onto my stomach and lay my head on her legs, looking up at her. "I'm sorry. I was shocked."

"I'm sorry I just blurted it out like that."

I run my fingers over her stomach. "I don't know if I'll be any good at it, but I'm gonna give it my best shot because . . . well, because I love you."

She gives another watery smile, resting her hand on my cheek. "I love you too."

"Then we'll do this. Together. And it'll be fine."

Hadley nods. "Together."

HADLEY

It's been a week since I found out about the pregnancy, and Grim's been true to his word. He's trying. He makes sure I'm eating and drinking and resting, even though I tell him it's not an illness and women get by every day doing this exact same thing. But he's being attentive and loving and all the things I need him to be to reassure me we're doing the right thing. Because I have my doubts. Not because I think Grim will make a terrible parent—I think he'll surprise himself on that front—but because this wasn't part of my life plan. I want kids, but in around five years, when my career is more established. My boss is great, she's a woman who believes in giving other women opportunities, but in law, men have dominated the career for too long and she prides herself on leading a strong female firm. Telling her won't mean she drops me from her team, and I'm pretty certain it won't affect my chances of promotion, but there's a niggling doubt I won't be able to do it all. And Grim might not be happy for me to have a full-time career and have his child. He's old fashioned and has already hinted about me staying home and becoming his ol' lady.

Mum places a cup of tea in front of me and joins me at the kitchen table. "You look troubled."

"Just tired," I say.

"You're working hard. Your boss would be crazy not to promote you."

"Everyone there works hard, we all deserve a promotion. Did you have a career before you had Mav?"

She scoffs. "Are you kidding? I met your father when I was far too young, and he swept me off my feet, told me I didn't need a career. Said he'd always provide for me if I looked after him."

"Didn't you want a career?"

"I wanted your father more." Her smile fades. "He was kind back then."

"Is it possible to have both, do you think?"

She nods. "Women do both all the time. Super women, if you ask me. I don't know how they juggle kids and jobs and taking care of the home. It's hard work." She sips her tea. "Why are you asking, Hadley?" I stare at her, waiting for her to catch on, and then her eyes widen. "Oh my god, you're not?" I nod. "Seriously? That's amazing!" She looks genuinely pleased. "Does Grim know?"

"Yeah. It wasn't planned, obviously, but he's coming around to the idea."

"I'm so pleased for the both of you."

"I'm dreading telling Meli. She's only just getting used to me and Grim being together and now this."

"She's your sister. She worries, but I think she'll be happy about this. She's going to be an aunt."

"Even after everything she's been through? It just feels so insensitive."

"Hadley, she loves you. She'll be thrilled."

CHAPTER FIFTEEN

GRIM

We sit around the table in church. Arthur and his brothers have joined us, which means he must have news on Cambridge.

"Arthur, you may as well start," says Mav glumly.

"Nick Cambridge has agreed to back away from Harriett. He's going to sign Ivy over to her for sole custody and he's paying her out. It's a good deal, and Harriett is happy to accept it."

"That's great," I say.

"Not entirely. He's made some additions to the agreement. He's going to take the target off your back."

"But?" asks Ghost.

"But he wants Grim to do time for what he did."

"Prison?" I snap. "Are you kidding?"

Arthur shakes his head. "No. That's his deal."

"Fuck his deal. I should have just killed him."

"Impossible now as he's made it known he's got issues with the club. His circle of elites is top judges, businessmen, men with power who know the right people. If you wade in there now and put a bullet in him, it'll come back on the club."

"Pres, I can't go to prison," I snap. The thought of Hadley bringing up my kid alone fills me with dread.

"Now you call me Pres," says Mav. "It won't come to that. We'll think of something else and re-negotiate."

"Good because I can't leave Hadley now."

"Why?" asks Ghost. I realise what I've said and stutter for an answer. Ghost smiles. "Fuck, you didn't get her pregnant?"

The room falls silent, and Mav's eyes burn into me. Hadley's gonna kill me. "Everyone out!" snaps Mav, and the room clears in seconds. "Get talking."

"Maybe we should go to the basement and fight first?"

"Grim, get talking."

"It was an accident."

He dives up, grabbing my shirt and hauling me to my feet. "What did you do, fall and stick your unwrapped dick in her?" he yells. "Fucking my sister without protection isn't an accident!" he growls.

"She missed her shot, man, it wasn't my fault."

He releases me, shoving me back into my chair. "You've been together only a few weeks," he snaps.

"Months," I correct. "We just kept it quiet."

"You hate kids."

I nod. "I know."

"And now you're gonna be a dad?"

"Scary, right?"

"Shit. Is Hadley okay?"

"I think so. It shocked us both, but she's handling it well."

He heads over to the drinks trolley in the corner of the room and pours us each a drink. "My sister and my best mate," he mutters to himself, shaking his head. "A fucking kid . . . I still feel like Hadley's a kid sometimes."

"She isn't, trust me," I say with a smirk.

He glares at me, unamused. "Well, at least you haven't run away," he points out, like he's somehow shocked and impressed all at once.

"Only cos I don't have a licence," I joke, and he laughs.

"This is huge for you."

I nod. "I know. Still processing it all. We haven't spoken about it since she told me. I think we're both too scared to frighten the other. And she's got this promotion at work she's trying to get. It's like she hasn't registered that she'll be a mum and won't have time to work."

Mav smirks. "You're an idiot if you tell her that. Women keep careers these days. You can't ask her to give it up."

"Who'll look after the kid?"

"You will. It's not like you're any use to me now that you can't ride," he jokes.

"So, you see why I can't go to prison?"

"Yeah. I wouldn't agree to that anyway, brother. You're a part of this club, and I wouldn't sell you out like that. We'll find a new agreement." He finishes his drink. "You need to claim my sister, Grim." His tone is serious.

"Next on my list, brother."

"Good. No time like the present. I'll gather everyone."

"Actually, I think Hadley wants to speak to Meli first," I lie. I don't know what Hadley wants to do about her twin. We haven't spoken about the baby or who we should tell, but I know without doubt, I have to be the one to tell Meli first.

"She needs to make it quick, tell her to do it now."

"Mav, come on, there's no rush on this. Let the girls work it out, and I'll give you the go ahead when it's right."

∞

I head straight for Meli's room, but as I get to the door, Hadley comes out of her own room, so I swerve Meli's and wrap my arms around Hadley, pushing her back inside the bedroom and kissing her. "I was coming to find you," I growl in her ear, pressing my erection against her.

"I told Mum," she blurts out, and my erection deflates.

"Okay. How did she take it?"

"Really well, actually."

I groan before confessing, "Mav knows too."

"Oh crap, how did he take it?"

I shrug. "Also really well. He wants to tell everyone."

"I thought he'd be mad."

"Can we lock ourselves away?" I ask, and she laughs.

"Why are we hiding this from everyone?" We should be holding our heads up and showing everyone how much we love each other."

"That brings me to my next announcement. How do you feel about being my ol' lady, officially?"

"Is that one of Mav's conditions?" Hadley asks.

"He did bring it up, but I was going to ask anyway. It was on my list."

She wraps her arms around my neck and kisses me. "Um, what else is on your list of things to do?"

HADLEY

I stare at my flushed reflection in the mirror and smile to myself. I don't remember the last time I felt so happy.

"I'll go grab us some food," shouts Grim from the bedroom.

"Wait," I say, running my fingers through my wavy hair, "I'll come too. I don't know what I want."

"This kid is making you fussy already," he complains.

I go into the bedroom. "It's making me greedy," I say, and he rubs a hand over my stomach.

"You're gorgeous," he whispers, kissing me on the head.

Downstairs, the bar is busy with brothers. "What's the occasion?" I ask Grim, and he shrugs, going off into the kitchen.

Mav takes my hand and kisses me on the cheek. "Congratulations, little sis," he says, smiling.

"Thank you. What's going on here tonight?"

"I wanted to announce the news, but Grim said to wait because you want to tell Meli."

I frown. "We haven't spoken about it, but seeing as it's out now, I don't mind you making an announcement."

"Are you sure, cos Meli is drinking and you know what she's like for drama."

I grin, watching my sister and Rosey knocking back shots and giggling. "Hopefully, she'll be happy for me."

"Get Grim. I'll make this lot shut the hell up."

I go into the kitchen and grab Grim by the hand. "Come, I want to show you something," I say.

The bar is silent when we return, and I lead Grim to the front where Mav is. "What's going on?" he whispers, and I wink. It makes a change for me to surprise him.

"I want to share two things tonight," Mav begins, "and I thought I'd do it quickly because we all know how Grim is when it comes to this sort of thing. Most of us had bets on him being the only bachelor to get to pension age without settling down, but it seems my little sister has the magic touch."

"Or a magic pu—" shouts Ghost.

Mav cuts him off. "Less of that talk, thanks. Grim's finally settling down, and I'm honoured it's with my sister, Hadley."

Meli has stood up and she's staring wide-eyed between me and Grim. I frown. It's not like she didn't know we're together, so why does she look so upset? "And he's taking a step further by making her his ol' lady," continues Mav. There's a few cheers and whistles, but Mav quietens them down again. "I haven't finished."

"Maybe that's enough big announcements for one day," whispers Grim uncomfortably.

I take his hand. "Let's go with it," I reply.

"It's not a good idea," he begins.

"Grim and Hadley are having a baby," says Mav. The noise from the brothers is almost deafening as they jump around, congratulating us. I'm swept up in the arms of different brothers, and when I look around for Grim, I spot him talking to Meli. She's upset, I can see it on her face, and I can't help but feel annoyed. I know she's been through some shit, but she can still be happy for me. I try to head to them, but Rylee hugs me, dragging my attention away from the pair.

GRIM

"Let's go talk," I mutter.

"There's not much left to say," whispers Meli, but it's obvious she's upset.

"I didn't know they were gonna tell everyone like this. I asked Mav to wait because I wanted to tell you first."

"Good of you," she mutters. Rosey shoves between us, looking angrily at me.

"You've got bloody nerve," she snaps. "If you weren't the VP, I'd slit your fucking throat."

"Well, I am the VP, so watch your mouth," I hiss. "Meli, please, let's talk."

"I don't want to talk to you, Grim. Leave me alone."

Hadley comes over, and I groan. She catches it and glares at me. "Sorry, am I interrupting?"

"Why did you let Mav do that tonight?" I snap. "I asked him to wait."

"I told him it was fine."

"Clearly, it isn't," says Rosey, smirking.

"Meli, I'm sorry you're upset, but I can't put my life on hold in case you don't approve," says Hadley.

Meli glares at me, arching her brow, urging me to speak up for her. "Hads, go easy," I mutter. "She's been through a lot."

"I know that," says Hadley, looking offended. "And I'm sorry you lost your baby, but I couldn't keep this a secret forever. It would hurt just as much six months down the line. I can't change it."

"Fuck this circus," I mutter. "Let's just go to bed."

Hadley frowns. "No, we're celebrating."

"I don't feel like celebrating anymore," I snap.

"Me either," mutters Meli, and she storms off towards the stairs.

I sigh. "I'm going to bed." I head off in the same direction, and once I get to the stairs, I take two at a time to catch Meli. She's about to go into her room, and I push my way in despite her protests. "I'm sorry, Amelia. Truly sorry."

"You're trying to ease your own conscience. Go away."

"Maybe I am, because I feel like a complete prick, but Hads falling pregnant was an accident."

"Just like me, right? Maybe it's time you started taking responsibility for your own actions. Try wrapping that thing so you don't accidentally get any other women pregnant."

"Those days are behind me. It's Hadley all the way. I love her."

Tears fill Meli's eyes. "Good for you."

"I just need to check you're not gonna—"

She scoffs. "Wow, seriously?"

"Are we still agreed that she shouldn't know?"

"Out of interest, what was it about her that lured you in?"

I shrug. "She was just there for me, listening and shit. We got to know each other."

"So, because I didn't stick around and hold you close after we fucked, I didn't stand a chance, right?"

I'm confused. "A chance?"

"Yes," she wails, throwing her hands in the air. "You're so fucking blind, Grim. Hadley spent years hoping you'd notice her, but you didn't. And then I give myself on a fucking plate and you don't even stick around to see what I have to offer!"

"I don't understand," I mutter.

"Of course, you don't. I thought if I played it cool, you'd respect it more and we'd naturally begin to like one another."

"No!" I gasp. "No, that's not possible. You made it clear we were just hooking up!"

"Of course, I did, because I thought you weren't ready!"

"This can't be happening," I mumble.

She wipes her eyes. "Forget I said anything. Congratulations. I hope you'll be very happy."

"Please don't be like that," I whisper, hooking my finger around hers and tugging her closer. "I'm so sorry." I wrap her in my arms, and she sobs into my chest.

"I can't stop thinking about the baby," she mumbles.

CHAPTER SIXTEEN

HADLEY

"Just tell me what the hell is going on," I say. Rosey has spent the last five minutes talking in my ear about what a mistake I'm making. "I feel like there's a reason you're saying all this, so just tell me."

"It's not up to me to say."

"It's not like you to keep your mouth shut," I snap. "Fine, I'll go and ask Meli because it's clearly a lot to do with her reaction."

Rosey shrugs. "I'm not saying a word, but I bet if you go up there now, she's not alone."

I hesitate, my heart slamming in my chest. "What's that supposed to mean?"

She shrugs again, and I growl in frustration before marching upstairs. Rosey is behind me, and as my hand lands on the door handle to Meli's room, I glance back at her. She nods, encouraging me to go inside. My heart is screaming at me to stop because something feels off, and I know whatever is behind this door is going to change everything.

I take a breath and push it open. Grim's back is to me, and Meli is in his arms sobbing while he strokes a hand down her hair. "It could have been us," she mumbles, not noticing her audience.

He kisses the top of her head and shushes her. I look at Rosey, and she gives me a sad, sympathetic smile.

"I knew you were upset, Meli, but this seems a little over the top, even for you." At my words, they break apart and Grim winces. "Don't let me break up whatever that was. What was that exactly?"

"Not what you think," Grim responds.

I nod slowly. "Good, cos what I was thinking was you seemed pretty cosy and not in the in-law kind of way but more in the 'we've had sex' kind of way."

"Oh, she's good," says Rosey from behind me.

Grim gives her an annoyed look. "I might have known you'd be behind this."

She smiles wide and curtsey's before him. "It was only a matter of time before your lying, cheating arse got caught, I just helped her join the dots."

"Rosey, get out," I order. She leaves without uttering a smart-arse comment for once. "The one-night stand?" I ask, looking mainly at Meli. She nods, looking guilty. I rub my chest, like that will somehow dull the pain there. Running my fingers through my hair, I take a few breaths to chase away the tears that threaten to fall.

"Hads, it's not—" Grim begins, but I hold my hand up.

"Don't dare insult me by saying it isn't how it seems. Did you two have sex?" He pleads to me with his eyes, but when he realises I'm waiting for him to respond, he finally nods. "When we were together?"

"Fuck, Hadley, no. What do you think I am?" he snaps.

My eyes widen in disbelief that he dares react like that. "Right now, I don't know who the fuck you are," I say, coldly. "How many times?"

"Twice," Meli answers before he can.

"So, not a one-night stand!" I point out angrily. "And you got pregnant. If she hadn't lost it, would you be with her?" I ask Grim.

"Don't do this. Let's go and talk properly."

"We're talking now so I get the full picture and not the parts you choose to give me!" I yell. "How could you let me make that announcement when you knew she'd lost your child," I cry, mortified.

"I tried to stop you. I told Mav to wait!" he yells back.

"You didn't try hard enough, and you should have told me right from the start!" I scream.

"She didn't fucking lose it, okay," he growls out. "She got rid of it."

I suck in a breath and take a shaky step back. "What?"

He glares at Meli, who begins crying harder. "She chose to have an abortion, and I supported that. We're not together. It was an accident."

"Like this is an accident?" I ask, rubbing a hand over my stomach.

"No, not like you and me," he says desperately. "I love you, Hadley, you know I do."

I shake my head and choke on my words. "If you loved me, Grim, you'd have told me right from the start that you'd slept with my twin sister."

Tears roll down my cheeks, and it makes me angry at myself for letting him see me upset, so I rush from the room. I can hear him telling Meli he'll be back as I slam my bedroom door, locking it right as he reaches it. He bangs his fists against it. "Let me in!" I sit on the edge of my bed and take deep breaths. "Hadley, fucking open the door so we can talk about this."

"When was the last time?" I ask.

"I can't remember. Before us . . . weeks before us."

"So why didn't you tell me?"

"What was the point? I was embarrassed and didn't want anyone to know. It was a hook-up, nothing else."

"Because you knew I wouldn't ever get with you, that's why!" I cry out.

"I'm not doing this through a door. We can talk about it like adults," he says firmly, and it fills me with rage. "I'm the VP. I can't stand out here begging."

"Don't pull rank on me. And if you want to talk about age, aren't you old enough to know better?"

"Open the door."

"God, I feel sick," I mumble to myself.

"Open the door!" He sounds angrier.

"Did you compare us? Isn't it every man's dream to sleep with twins?"

"Hadley, open the fucking door," he yells, and it's followed by a loud crack. My bedroom door swings open and the lock falls to the ground. Grim fills the doorway, his fists clenched and his shoulders square, like he's ready for a fight.

Vomit threatens to leave my stomach and I rush to the bathroom. Grim sticks his foot in the door before I can lock that, but I'm in too much of a rush to make a fuss as I drop to my knees and spill the contents of my stomach into the toilet. I feel his hand on my back and I swat it away. After a few minutes of sickness, I grab some toilet tissue and wipe my mouth.

Grim slides down the door, sitting opposite me. "Do you need anything?"

"Yes, a man who doesn't lie to me."

"I was thinking more drink or food?" He tries to joke, but I don't laugh. He can't talk me round with wisecracks and cheeky smiles.

"Whose idea was it to keep it a secret from me?" I whisper.

"I don't really remember. Mutual, I guess."

"The day you disappeared, the weird behaviour, the sudden talk of getting our own place, that was the problem that was sending you crazy?"

He nods and looks at his hands, twisting his club ring around his finger. "She asked me to stay away from you, and I tried, but it was hard. I missed you, and Mav gave me this talk about you and how you're good for me, and I thought, fuck it, if Mav approves, I don't care what Meli thinks." He rests his head back against the wall and closes his eyes. "You make everything feel better, and I wasn't ready to walk away. The more time we spent together, the harder it got. When she told me she was pregnant, my first thought wasn't about Meli or even the baby—it was how the fuck I was gonna tell you. I didn't talk her out of the abortion because it meant I could keep us a secret and then I wouldn't lose you."

"You should know by now that nothing is a secret in this club. It always comes out in the end."

"I told her we were together, and she was upset but agreed it wouldn't serve any good if we told you. We were done, a fling, and it wasn't worth losing you over."

"So, you kept it a secret and now look what's happened."

"It was a mistake. I should have told you right from the beginning, I see that now."

"Now, you've been caught." I stand and take my toothbrush, and Grim watches from the floor as I brush my teeth. "You need to leave," I mutter before rinsing my mouth.

He shakes his head. "I'm not leaving you alone."

"You promised Meli you'd go back to her," I say coldly. He follows me back into my room, watching as I get undressed. It's still early, but I'm exhausted, and all I want to do is curl up in my bed and forget today ever happened. I pick his shirt up, the one I usually wear for bed, and hold it, feeling the soft cotton in my fingers. My heart squeezes in my chest, and I drop it to the floor and get a nightshirt of my own from the drawer. I also get clean sheets because I don't want to smell him in my bed or on my skin, the thought causing me to shudder.

"What are you doing?" he asks, trying to take the sheets from me. I move around him and begin stripping the bed. "Hadley," he pleads.

"It hurts too much," I mutter. "Your smell was a comfort before, but now—" A painful noise leaves my throat involuntary.

He nods sadly and begins to change the bed for me. When it's done, I climb under the covers and turn my back to him, praying he'll leave me alone. He doesn't, and I hear him walk over to the chair by the window.

I can't take the million questions racing around my mind, so after a long silence, I eventually ask, "Did you hold her?" I'm not sure why I go with that question over so many others, like whether he enjoyed it or whether he had a better time with her.

"Huh? No. No, I told you, it wasn't like that."

"You listened to me rant about the man who got my sister pregnant. You suggested it was probably a random guy she met." I groan. "God, I'm such a twat."

"Hadley, you're not. Don't say that."

"It would have bothered me, and I'd never have gotten with you had I known from the start, but the fact you went to such lengths to hide it, hurts me way more."

"I panicked."

"When you made me promise not to leave you, was it because of this?"

"You promised to stay," he mutters.

"It was before I knew about this," I snap. "I didn't know what I was promising, but you did, and you still asked me, knowing what that meant for me, for us."

∞

I lie awake for hours. The pain in my heart won't let me sleep despite how exhausted I am. Hurt begins to turn to anger around two in the morning and I look over to see Grim sleeping peacefully. I'm jealous he can sleep so easily, so fucking guilt-free now his dirty little secret isn't weighing heavy on his mind. I get out of bed and head downstairs.

I'm making myself a hot chocolate when the door opens and I'm face-to-face with Meli. Her eyes are red and swollen, and it's obvious she's been crying. "Oh, sorry," she whispers. "I thought everyone would be in bed."

"For some reason, I couldn't sleep," I say, my voice dripping with sarcasm.

"Hadley, I am so sorry," she says desperately. "I wanted to tell you, I told him to tell you, but he was worried it would ruin everything."

"He was right to be worried."

"Don't say that. You've liked him for so long, and now you've finally got him. Don't let something so little like this ruin it."

"Little?" I snap. "This isn't little, Meli. Why do you both keep playing it down? My boyfriend had sex with my twin sister—it sounds like a fucking chat show topic!"

"It didn't mean anything."

"Bullshit. Did he ask you to get rid of the baby?"

She shakes her head. "No."

"But I'm guessing he didn't try to stop you either."

"No, but he was really nice. He asked more than once if I was sure, and he was really great at the clinic. He—"

"Grim went with you?" She hesitates before nodding, and I groan. It was the right thing to do on his part, but it leaves me feeling even more in the dark. "There's been this whole big cover-up and I didn't see it. I feel like an idiot."

"We didn't mean to make you feel like that."

"You don't get it," I snap. "I've watched him for years, and his eyes have always been on you. And then suddenly, he looked my way, and he said all the things I've been wanting to hear. He made all the right promises. Then to find out he had sex with you, his perfect woman, it hurts me. It makes me doubt everything he ever said. And to top it off, you knew how much I liked him, and you still went there."

"I know," she mumbles, looking down at the ground. "But I was certain he was never gonna be with you, so I didn't see the harm."

I scoff. "Right, because he's so out of my league?"

"God, no, that's not what I meant. You're out of his, Hadley. You can do way better."

"This is going nowhere," I say, sighing. "It doesn't matter why you did what you did or even that you knew how I felt. It doesn't matter that it was before I officially got with him. It matters that you both lied to me and planned to keep that up. I might never have found out, and I would have spent a life with a man that had sex with my twin." I shudder. "It makes me sick to my stomach."

"Hadley, you're pregnant, and he made you his ol' lady. He loves you. He told me he loves you. Please don't throw it away over this."

"I can't see a way around it, Meli. I can't even look at him, and I don't want to look at you. I feel so fucking hurt." As I go to leave, I pause beside her. "Answer me one thing. Does Rosey know everything?" Her guilty expression tells me yes without her having to say a word.

I slap her. It shocks us both as she grips her cheek, and her eyes fill with tears again. I turn, colliding with Mav's chest. "Somebody explain."

"Not here," I mutter, pushing past him and rushing to his office. He follows, and as we go inside, I turn to Meli. "Not you." I slam the door.

Mav stares, open-mouthed. "You hit her?"

"She deserved it."

"From the beginning," he demands.

"Grim slept with her."

Mav almost chokes. "What?"

"The baby she supposedly lost was his. She terminated the pregnancy while he held her hand." I wince at the pain of those words as they burn my throat.

Mav drops in his office chair and stares at me in shock. "He wouldn't," he eventually mumbles.

"Well, he did, Mav. He slept with my twin and then—" I burst into tears, and he rushes towards me, wrapping me in his arms. "I feel so fucking betrayed," I sob out. He holds me for a few minutes while I fight to get myself under control.

"This happened before you, after you, or while you were . . ." He releases me and heads back to his seat, pulling out a bottle of vodka and drinking directly from the bottle.

"It happened before me and him, but the lies have continued since. He didn't plan on telling me. Neither of them did. Our announcement today raised suspicions and I worked it out." I stare up at the ceiling, groaning aloud. "What a fucking mess."

"At least no one knows."

"Except Rosey." I shrug bitterly. "Seems Rosey gets to know everything these days."

"Hadley, I'm so sorry," Mav mutters. "I told him to go for it with you. If I'd have known."

"Don't worry, this isn't your fault."

"I'll fucking kill him!"

I shake my head. "He's your VP. The brothers come first, and you shouldn't get involved in love disputes," I say, forcing a smile. "Isn't that the rules?"

"I'm not sure the rules apply when he's broken a few himself."

CHAPTER SEVENTEEN

GRIM

I'm awoken by something hitting me on the head. I sit up, groaning from the aches in my body after sleeping in this damn chair. The first thing I see is a boxing glove flying towards my head. I catch it, frowning, then I see Mav is staring at me and he's mad. It's clear by the pulsing vein in his forehead and his clenched jaw. "Let's go, Romeo."

"That depends where we're going," I say, dread filling me.

"You don't get to ask questions."

He leaves the room. I scoop up the other glove from the ground and follow him as we head straight for the basement. Once inside, he locks the door. "Special date with my Pres or time for me to meet Hades?" I ask cautiously.

His fist catches me hard in the stomach and I wince, doubling over and coughing violently. "I said no fucking questions!" he yells. "Tell me why I shouldn't put a bullet in your skull right now!"

"Do it. I deserve it."

"Damn right you deserve it. Who even are you? I sure as hell don't know this version."

"I don't have an excuse," I say, still doubled over. "I've always been a dick."

"Drop the gloves, we don't need 'em."

I chuck them into the corner and straighten up. "We doing this the old-fashioned way?"

"Hit me," Mav orders.

I shake my head. "No."

"Hit me, Grim. I can't lay into you until you do." I hesitate, and he shoves me backwards. "Hit me," he growls out.

I groan. "Still a gentleman even after I fucked both your sisters," I mutter. It's low, but I won't hit my President and I know this will have the desired effect.

He growls, shoving me harder this time. I hit the wall, and he brings his fist back but holds it there. "Why?"

"Because I don't know how to say no. Because I'm a fucked-up piece of shit. Because I could!"

That tips him over the edge. I don't fight back when he lays into me, taking every punch, choking on my own blood until I'm on the ground. I hear a banging on the door, then he stops, breathless. "Even after everything, she still asked me not to get involved," he spits out in disgust. "She still fucking defended you."

Mav unlocks the door, and Hadley rushes in. She gasps at the sight of me. "I told you I wouldn't kill him, but I made no promises about hurting him," says Mav coolly before walking out.

Hadley stares at me for a few seconds, a range of emotions passing over her face before she leaves too. That hurts worse than the punches.

Ghost comes in and winces. "Ouch." Holding out his hand for me to grab, I shout out in pain as he pulls me to stand. "Ribs?" he asks, and I nod. "He always goes for the ribs."

"Does everyone hate me?" I mutter, limping from the basement.

"Since when do brothers involve themselves in ol' lady drama? It isn't our business. I will say, we all love Hads and Meli, and it was a shit thing you did, but then you already know that."

∞

While Mum sits watching, Mama B cleans me up. She isn't gentle about it, and I don't blame her. "Proud of me, Ma?" I ask sarcastically. It's not her I'm mad at, it's myself, but she's an easy target.

She lowers her eyes. "Do you need me to answer that?"

Mama B hits me around the head. "Show some fucking respect in my kitchen." I try to remember the time she got her balls, because when Eagle was around, she was quiet as a mouse. "Make this right, Grim. I don't care how you do it, just do it."

I drag my tired, aching body upstairs to Hadley's room and knock on the door before going inside. She's sitting cross-legged on her bed, staring blankly at the wall. "Penny for them," I whisper.

"Does it hurt?" she asks.

"Yes."

"Good."

"Can we talk?"

"I'm going to talk, and you can listen," she says, pointing for me to sit in the chair, which I do. "I knew there would always be a possibility getting involved with you would end in my heart being broken," she says, "I never for one minute thought it would be because you had sex with my twin."

"I don't know how to make it right."

She shakes her head sadly. "That's the thing . . . you can't."

"What are you saying?" My heart speeds up.

"I've thought about it, it's all I've thought about. There's no way I can ever forgive you. I'll never get past this."

I rush to her side and grab her hand. "You don't mean that, Hads. It takes time, and I'll make it up to you, I promise."

She pulls her hand free. "You can't. I'd always wonder if you're thinking of her when you were with me. I've spent my life living in Meli's shadow, and I won't do it anymore."

"I don't think of her," I say desperately. "We weren't together, not like we are. I feel it with you, Hadley. I love you."

"It's not love, Grim. If it was, you'd have been honest from the start. Instead, you kept it from me and let me fall for you."

"We're having a baby," I say, placing my hand over her stomach.

Her eyes fill with tears, and she pushes my hand away. "Don't touch me. It makes my skin crawl." She takes a deep breath. "I've thought about it, and I can't be around you and Meli right now, so I'm moving out."

"No!" I snap. "No way! This is your home. I'll leave."

"You're the Vice President, it's not practical."

"I don't think Mav will stop me, Hadley."

"And Meli? I'm making this easy on us all. My boss said I can stay with her for now."

"What about the baby?" I ask.

"I haven't thought about the baby just yet. I'm still getting through this part. I'll be in touch about that when I've got my head straight."

∞

I knock on Mav's office door, and he narrows his eyes when he sees it's me. "What?"

"Hadley wants to leave the clubhouse."

"Over my fucking dead body. No one's going anywhere."

"I have a solution."

"And why would I listen to anything you've got to say?"

"Because it means Hadley can stay here."

I slowly lower onto the couch, holding my ribs. Mav smirks. "Call Arthur, tell him to speak to Cambridge, and tell him he's got himself a deal.""What?"

"What's the worst I'll get, two years? I can do two years."

"It's not a good idea," mutters Mav, shaking his head.

I smile. "I know you'll miss me, brother, but it's for the best. You know it is. You can't kick me out over this and you can't let Hadley leave, so I'll go away for a while and let the dust settle. When I get out, things will be different."

"And what about the club?"

"You know as well as I do, my head's been fucked for months. All the shit that went down over Meli and Ripper. Rosey coming back. Crow. Mum being a mess. I just need time and so does Hadley."

"And when you come home?"

"I'll claim my ol' lady."

Mav laughs. "You got nerve. Hadley won't forgive you for this."

"Maybe not, but I'm not giving up on her. You told me when you weren't with Rylee, you felt like you were wading through the dark, right?" He nods. "And that's exactly how Hadley makes me feel, Mav. I love her. I fucked up not telling her about Meli, but it wasn't even a thing, and I wasn't planning on falling for Hads. It just happened, but by then, it was too late. I was scared to lose her. I know what I did was messed up, but it wasn't intentional. So I'll go to prison, but she's always gonna be mine. I'll never give up."

Mav smirks. "You got balls, I'll give you that. What if she meets someone before you get out?"

"You won't let that happen."

"Confident too. Brother, I'll make sure she meets someone worth ten of you."

I stand and head over to the table where the vodka is, pouring us each a glass. "I let you beat me. Fuck, I'm even pissing blood. But you're still my President. You're still my brother, and most of all, you're still my best mate. We've been through too much to give up on each other now." He takes the drink and we clink glasses. "I'm sorry, Pres. Truly. I didn't mean to let you down or hurt her. I'll make up for it."

HADLEY

I open my bedroom window and take in the fresh, cool breeze. It's been a week since Grim's secret floored me. And three days since I left the club and moved in with

Amanda, my boss. It's different here, quiet, but it's not as bad as I thought. Amanda is never around. She works all the hours she can, and when she isn't at the office, she's in her home study working or her gym in the basement. So, basically, I have the run of the place.

My phone buzzes and I roll my eyes when I see Grim's name. He's left me alone up until now, respecting my wishes for once. I leave it for the answer message to pick up, but he rings right back, so I answer. "Don't hang up," he begs. "Please, can I come and see you?"

"No."

"It's really important, Hads. I wouldn't ask if it wasn't. And I literally have about an hour."

"Until?"

"Meet me. The bar I took you to, the one I love to go to alone."

∞

I know I shouldn't go, he doesn't deserve my time, but I can't switch off my heart and part of me longs to catch a glimpse of him. Being strong is hard when you're so alone.

The bar is just as lifeless as the last time I was here. Grim is staring at the door as I enter. He smiles, but I don't return it. "Make it quick," I mutter, taking a seat.

He looks nervous. "How have you been?"

"Tired, heartbroken, sick."

He nods, wincing at my words. "Morning sickness?"

"What do you want?"

"I miss you so much," he begins, and I stand to leave. This isn't what I came for. He grabs my hand. "Sorry, don't go." I sigh heavily and sit back down. "I'm going away for a while." I finally meet his eyes. They're still bruised from Mav's punches, but he looks deadly serious. "I'd really like it if you'd go back home to the club while I'm away. It's safer there."

"Where are you going?"

"It's not important. I'll be gone for maybe a year or two. Will you go back home?"

I shrug. The thought of being around Meli is hard. "Tell me where you're going."

He grabs my hand, and I stare at it like it's poison. Truth is, it hurts my heart because I want to hold onto him so tight, but then I remember where his hands have been, and it makes me sick. "I know you're hurting, and I hate myself for being the reason for that. But I love you, despite what you think. You're everything to me, and I can't let you go. So, I'll go away for a while and give you time to heal. But when I come home, I will prove to you how much you mean to me. I won't ask you to wait because that's unfair, but just know, if you meet anyone else, it won't stop me coming back for you and our baby."

"Please," I whisper, my eyes begging him to stop, "I can't listen to this now."

"I just had to tell you before I go."

The door opens and four police officers enter. Grim smiles at them. "Right on time," he mutters bitterly.

"What have you done?" I hiss.

"Hudson Grimes?" asks one of the officers.

"Yep," mutters Grim, standing.

"You need to come with us."

"Grim?" I ask, wanting him to explain what the hell is going on.

His blue eyes burn into mine and he smiles as an officer pulls his hands behind his back and begins to read him his rights. "I'm coming back for you, Hadley. I love you, and you're always gonna be my ol' lady. Don't forget that."

"What are you arresting him for?" I demand to know.

The officer cuffs his hands. "Suspected assault."

"I'm his solicitor," I say, grabbing my bag.

"No," says Grim, and I stop. "Not this time, baby. I got this."

They lead him from the bar, and I watch helplessly as Mav steps inside. "What's going on?" I demand.

"It's what he wanted. He made a deal with Cambridge. I tried to talk him out of it."

"Well, I'll go and represent him. We'll get him out of it."

Mav shakes his head. "He doesn't want you to. He chose this, so let him do it his way. You both need time apart."

"I don't need time apart, Mav. It doesn't matter how long he stays away, I won't forgive him."

"I know that, I told him the same thing, but he's a stubborn arse, always thinking he knows best."

"He's sending himself away for no reason because it isn't going to work."

"If you hate him so much, why do you look so devastated?" he asks with a sad smile. "Come home, Hadley. We miss you."

I shake my head. "Not yet. I'm not ready."

"You belong at the club. You're safer there."

I gather my bag and coat. "I just need time, Maverick. Plenty of time."

CHAPTER EIGHTEEN

HADLEY

16 months later . . .

I rest against the oak tree, watching Meli swing my giggling eight-month-old daughter around in circles. It's hard to believe she's eight months old already—the time seems to have flown by. From the minute I held Oakley in my arms after a long, painful labour, I knew I'd do anything to protect her. The feeling of love was so overwhelming that I couldn't bear to keep Meli out of our lives a second longer. I wanted her to feel what I felt for the newest addition to our family, so I made the decision to forgive her. It wasn't easy. Even now, there are times when I look at her and feel a small stab of pain. But she's an amazing aunty and worships Oakley more than anyone.

"I gotta go," shouts Mav, and Meli kisses Oakley on the head. I take my daughter and do the same, before walking towards Mav and handing her over. "Any message?" he asks, the way he always does.

I shake my head. I might have forgiven Meli, but I'm having a hard job doing the same for Grim. That's why, every two weeks, Mav and Mum take Oakley to see him in prison. He shouldn't miss being a part of her life because he's an idiot, but I can't bring myself to face him. And, as if the lies and secrets weren't painful enough, I felt like he took the easy option by handing himself over to the cops and going away to prison. He was handed a three-year prison sentence. I didn't need any more details. Knowing he was out of our lives for three years was enough.

I moved back into the club right before I gave birth. Mainly because Mum begged me. She hated being apart from me and laid the Mum guilt on thick.

Grim's written to me every week. The same words. 'To my ol' lady, I love you. I'll always love you. Forgive me.' After six months, I didn't bother to open them. Instead, I placed them in a shoebox under my bed. Mav must have told him because then he started writing letters to Oakley, knowing I'd open them. Those letters were harder to read. They were heartfelt and full of regret. Mum talked me into letting her take Oakley to visit him in prison when she turned eight weeks old. When he writes to her, he tells her how much he loves her and talks about the milestones he's missing by being apart from her. He tells her how he's reading books in the prison library about parenting because he wants to be the best dad to her, just like his dad was to him.

It hurts me to read them, but I do it for her each night instead of her bedtime story, and I know she's too young to understand, but I guess he wants her to know why he missed these important years of her life. These letters leave no doubt how much he misses her and how he thinks about her every single day.

I asked Mav once if Grim was good with Oakley. He'd always been awkward around kids and made no secret of the fact he didn't really like them. So, when Mav smiled wide and nodded, I was surprised. "He's amazing with her, better than most dads I've watched. It's like the rest of the world fades out and it's just him and her in the room alone."

I cried after I heard that. Mainly because I was happy Oakley had another person to love her exactly like I did. A small part of me worried he'd not bother with her and his insistence on seeing her every fortnight was part of a plan to win me over.

My phone rings, bringing me from my daydream. I wave as Mav drives out of the club parking lot, then I answer my phone. "Good morning," says Harry.

"Good morning to you too."

"I was wondering if you'd meet me for lunch today."

I check my watch. "I guess I could squeeze you in," I tease. "I have some work to catch up on, so is twelve okay?"

We settle on that, and I head inside to do some work. It's Saturday, but since getting my promotion, I've been given almost double the caseload and I work every spare minute I get.

It's eleven when Mav walks in followed by Mum. When I spot neither of them are holding Oakley in their arms, I stand, feeling a panic rushing through me. "Relax," says Mav with a smile.

Mum mouths the word 'sorry' before the doorway is filled with Grim and Oakley. I stare. There are no words because my mouth is suddenly dry and my heart squeezes before beating wildly in my chest.

There's a rush of brothers pouring through as word travels around the club that Grim is home, and I watch them greet him like he's a returning hero. I feel a hand slip into mine. It's Rylee, and she leads me from the room and into the kitchen.

"He's out early?" I ask, lowering into a seat in shock.

"Mav didn't tell me. I would have come straight to warn you if I knew." She hands me a glass of water. "Are you okay?"

I nod slowly. "It was a shock, that's all."

"How did he get early release? He's been in trouble more than once in there," asks Rylee, thinking out loud.

"He has?"

"Fighting mainly," she says, shrugging. I'd never asked about him because the less I spoke about him, the more I could pretend he was in my past.

The door opens and I tense, refusing to look back. I already know it's him because of Rylee's expression. "Hadley," he says, and I briefly close my eyes. I've missed his voice.

"Do you want me to go?" asks Rylee.

"If that's okay," says Grim. She waits for me to respond, and I eventually nod. "I asked Mama B to watch Oakley for a minute." He moves into my eyeline, but I don't look up, scared of how I'll feel when I look into those blue eyes that have haunted my dreams for months. "You look amazing," he says, taking a seat opposite me. His scent fills my nostrils, and I take a drink of water to distract myself. "How have you been?"

I take a moment to think over his question. How have I been? Lost, lonely, sad, hurt. "Fine," I mutter.

"That's good. Did you get my letter? I told you I was meeting the parole board today and there was a chance I'd get released." I shake my head. Fuck, why didn't I read the letters? "I thought you might not read them. I guess I deserve that."

I glance at my watch. "Fuck," I mutter to myself. "Sorry, I have to go." I stand, feeling his eyes on me.

"Can't it wait? I haven't seen you in over a year." "Sorry," I repeat, rushing from the room.

GRIM I watch Hadley leave the kitchen and sigh. I don't know what I expected. Sixteen months felt like five years to me, and I thought about Hadley and Oakley every second of those months. Maybe that's why time dragged on. But I dreamt of seeing her and how she'd forgive me, throwing herself in my arms and telling me how much she missed me. I didn't prepare myself for the look of horror on her face or the way she'd avoid looking at me. I should have guessed it wouldn't be easy, that's why she didn't visit or respond to my letters.

I head back to the main room because at least the brothers are pleased to see me. Ghost shoves a beer in my hand and the club girls push each other to sit beside me. "How come you got out early?" he asks.

"And why the fuck didn't you tell us?" asks Mav.

I wrote it in my letter to Hadley, but I suspected she wasn't reading them. The fact Mav didn't mention it when I called him last night confirmed my suspicions. It's why I'd called to arrange Mav's visit today. I was waiting at the gates the second he pulled up outside.

"I didn't wanna give you guys a chance to arrange a party," I say. "We all know how they end."

"You're not getting out of it that easily," says Copper. "It's tradition, and we'll party all night." I force a smile. All I want to do is be with Hadley until she forgives me. "And seeing as you've been missing for so long, I'll even give you first pick of the girls," he adds, and the club girls giggle.

Hadley rushes past me, and I watch her go to Oakley and kiss her on the head. She speaks briefly to her mum, who nods and smiles. Then Hadley leaves. I put my beer down and race after her, catching her as she gets to her car. "Where are you going?"

"I have lunch plans," she says, still not looking at me.

"Look at me, Hads," I demand. Eventually, she pulls her eyes to me. "We need to talk," I say firmly.

"We don't."

"Of course, we do. We have so much to talk about, including Oakley."

Her mobile rings and she winces when she looks at the screen. "I have to go, I'm running late."

I stare at the name flashing on the screen. It's a man. "You've met someone?"

"I'm not doing this now." She gets in the car and starts the engine.

I tug the passenger door open. "Then when?" I ask.

She drives away without answering, forcing me to slam the door closed. Cracking Hadley will be harder than I thought.

I turn to find Mum watching. When I reach her, I kiss her on the cheek, and she smiles sadly. "Hadley hasn't told anyone, but she meets him a few times a week."

"How do you know?" I ask, frowning.

"I just watch. Sometimes I overhear conversations, telephone calls. I'm good at staying in the shadows," she says, and I smile. I'm proud of her for staying clean. I expected her to slip back into old ways without me around, but it made her more determined to be there for me. We spent her visits learning about each other again and sometimes it was painful. But we're getting through it, and hopefully, now I'm free, we can talk about finding Xzavier and making things right. "It's Oakley's nap time," she adds.

Inside, I take my daughter from Mama B and head to the kitchen with Mum to make a bottle. While I was in prison, I attended every parenting class I could to learn all this stuff, but now, making a bottle for real feels totally different, and as I rock her in my arm and scoop powder into the plastic container, I feel nervous. Mum smiles reassuringly, standing back and allowing me to do it myself. I test the temperature just like I've been shown and then head upstairs to my room. Sitting on my bed, which smells freshly made, probably by the ol' ladies, I cradle Oakley in my arms and watch her feed.

It's hard to believe I helped create such a perfect little human. She has my bright blue eyes and Hadley's brown hair. She's chilled just like her mum, and as her eyes drift closed, I shuffle down on the bed and close my eyes too.

HADLEY

Lunch went by in a blur. I can't recall anything that Harry spoke about because my mind was racing. And each time he asked if I was okay, I lied and told him I had a headache. Eventually, it was over and I rushed back to the club, not really sure why I felt the need to be here because I don't want to see Grim, but I don't want to be away from him either.

Mama B smiles when I go looking for Oakley. "Grim took her upstairs for her nap." That sentence alone freaks me out. I've been her sole carer for her entire life, and now I'll have to share that with Grim. I don't know how to feel about that.

When she isn't in my room, in her cot beside my bed, I head for Grim's room. Standing in the doorway, I take in the scene before me. Oakley sleeping soundly in Grim's arms is the best yet most painful thing I've witnessed. As if he senses me there, he opens his eyes. They fix me with that cool expression he uses when he's trying to remain calm. "Was lunch good?"

"Yes," I lie. "I like her to sleep in her cot," I add.

"I'd know that if you stuck around to talk to me instead of meeting him."

I shouldn't feel guilty, I haven't done anything wrong, but it's hard not to when he's staring at me accusingly. I hadn't told anyone about Harry, mainly because it's new. He'd spent a long time asking me out, and I'd always turned him down. When it was clear my pregnancy wasn't putting him off, I began to think about him more. So, last month when he invited me to join him for lunch, I bit the bullet and said yes. We've had a handful of dates since then but nothing more, not even a kiss. I'm cautious about who I let into my heart these days, but Harry's been a completely understanding gentleman.

"I'll meet you outside by the tree," I mutter, lifting Oakley carefully from his arms and taking her to my room.

He's pacing when I join him outside. "I didn't expect you to wait for me," he begins.

"Good."

"But I can't deny I'm shocked."

"That someone would want me?" I ask, arching a brow.

"Don't be ridiculous. I dunno, I thought you'd be busy with Oakley and—"

"How fucking dare you," I hiss. "Don't judge me when you know nothing about me."

"Who looks after her when you're with him?" he snaps. "Has he met her?"

"I'm not talking about this with you, Grim. You've been back a few hours and you want to start laying down laws? It doesn't work like that. You wanted to talk about Oakley."

"I want to be part of her life," he mutters. "All of it."

"Of course."

"Bedtimes, bath times, dinner times, everything."

"Okay."

"Can we be around each other for that?"

I nod. "If you stay out of my private life. We can parent Oakley, but that's it."

He keeps his eyes to the ground. "You're my ol' lady."

I shake my head. "No, I'm not."

"Always. I'm not giving up on us."

"Meli's free and single still. Maybe she'll take you back."

I try to walk away, but I'm pulled back by my arm and pressed against the oak tree. He pushes his face to mine, and his whole body is pressed against mine. "I love you, you're mine, and I'll get you back."

"I have someone," I say firmly, ignoring the way my body pulls towards him.

He grips my left hand, holding it up between us. He places a gentle kiss against my finger. "I don't see no ring on it, baby. He should have snapped you up when he had the chance. Now, he's got to fight to keep you away from me."

I pull my hand free, and he smirks, his eyes staring deep into mine. I refuse to look away and back down, so I square my shoulders. His eyes flick to my lips, and I run my tongue over them without thinking. He smiles. "Fuck, I've missed those lips." He presses his thumb over my lower lip, then drags it along my jaw and loosely grips my neck. "We're not raking up the past, Hads. Warn your man I'm coming to claim what's mine." He presses a chaste kiss to the corner of my mouth, then releases me, walking back towards the clubhouse.

I stare after him, butterflies racing around my stomach. "Be strong, Hadley, you're not his whore," I hiss to myself. "Christ, you're the mother of his child and you deserve better."

CHAPTER NINETEEN

GRIM

As far as club parties go, this is the wildest I've seen it since Eagle was in charge. The ol' ladies and other women have gone to bed, leaving club girls and brothers drinking. My blurred vision homes in on Ghost bending Skye over the pool table and fucking her, and I snigger. Mav must be in his office cos he doesn't stand for that sort of thing unless it's in the privacy of the bedrooms. A hand runs over my thigh, then Star lowers onto my lap. She grinds against me until my cock is bursting through my jeans. "Sixteen months is a long time, VP," she whispers, and I nod. "Why don't you let me help you out?"

I grip her waist to stop her rubbing against me. "I have an ol' lady."

"Oh, cos Skye asked Hadley and she said you were free and single. We didn't wanna step on anyone's toes."

I shake my head, smirking. "She's mistaken."

I stand, almost tipping her to the floor. I head for bed, but as I get to Hadley's floor, I find myself feeling along the wall and stopping outside her room. If I want her to forgive me, I have to put myself in her life until she can't deny how she feels, so I push the door open and slip inside.

It's the most beautiful sight seeing Hadley curled up with her hand in Oakley's cot, her finger gripped tightly by our sleeping daughter. I take a seat in the armchair by her bed and relax. It's comfier than a prison bed, and I have no trouble drifting to sleep.

When I open my eyes, it's morning and there's no sign of Hadley or Oakley. I go to my own room to shower and dress. When I get downstairs to the dining room, Hadley is at the table with Rylee on one side and a prospect on the other. I nod for him to move which he does and I slip in his seat. Hadley narrows her eyes. "Morning, ol' lady," I say, winking. She ignores me. "I thought we could take Oakley out for the day."

"No."

I take Oakley from her highchair and cover her in kisses. "Maybe the park?"

"I said no."

"I heard, but we're still going out for the day, so choose or I will."

"I'm busy."

"With lover boy?"

She rolls her eyes, and Rylee glances at Hadley. "Lover boy?" she asks.

"Oh fuck, haven't you told anyone?" I ask, amused. Hadley's face flushes with embarrassment. "Is he a secret?"

"Only you keep secrets around here," she utters.

Meli walks in, blanking me and cooing over my shoulder at Oakley. It's awkward, but I pretend I haven't noticed Meli and go back to staring at Hadley. "So, where shall we take Oakley?"

"I'm busy," she hisses with more conviction this time.

"No, you're not. I'll get Oakley ready while you dress." I stand, and Meli steps back. She catches my eye and gives a small smile as I pass her to head upstairs. If I want to win her sister over, I have to avoid Meli.

I'm changing Oakley when Hadley comes in. "You take her, I'll make up some bottles."

"Don't you trust yourself around me?" I ask, not taking my eyes off Oakley. "Are you scared I might actually win you back?"

"Don't be ridiculous."

"Then get dressed, Hadley, because we're spending our first day as a family and you're coming."

Half an hour later, I'm pushing Oakley in her stroller with Hadley by my side. I can't keep the smile from my face. It's exactly what I thought about on the nights I wanted to give up. "Tell me about her birth," I say, and Hadley looks taken back. "I wrote and asked, but you didn't write back. I've thought about it a lot and wondered how my baby girl came into the world."

"I don't really remember it," she mutters.

"Liar. How long were you in labour?"

"Twelve hours."

"I bet you were calm," I say, smiling.

"Actually, no, I wasn't. I panicked, and Mum had to keep me calm until I got to the hospital. I felt like something bad was going to happen and I couldn't shake it. It wasn't until I held her in my arms that I felt like I could breathe."

I hate that I wasn't there to comfort her when she needed me. "Did you have pain relief?"

"Gas and air. Mum was great, really calm."

"I hate I wasn't there."

"Even if you weren't in prison, you wouldn't have been there, Grim."

I laugh, amused by her strong act. "Of course, I would have been. Who the fuck would have stopped me being at the birth of my daughter? Why didn't you read my letters?"

"What was the point?"

"I just needed you to know I was thinking about you. Did you think about me?"

"No," she lies, and I smile again.

"It hurt you didn't visit or write. I thought you might come on Oakley's first visit."

She sighs heavily. "Why would I? We weren't together."

"Of course, we were," I say. "I fucked up, but it's done now, and we have Oakley to think about."

"You can't just decide we're together, Grim. You fucked up, and I left you. That's it. End of story."

"What about when Oakley asks why we aren't together?"

"I'll tell her you fucked Aunty Meli and I couldn't move past it," she hisses.

I stop abruptly and grip her chin between my fingers. "It was before us. I didn't cheat."

"You may as well have," she whispers.

"But I didn't. The only thing I did was keep it from you, and for that I'm sorry, but it's over with now. You have to move forward. You've forgiven her, so why not me?"

"She's my sister."

"And I'm the father of your baby."

"Unfortunately."

"You're kidding yourself. I know you love me, I can see it in your eyes," I say, smirking.

She pulls away and begins walking in front. We get to the park, and she takes a seat on a wooden bench and pulls out her phone.

HADLEY

Just because Grim forced me to join him today doesn't mean I'm going to play happy family. I'm reading my emails from work when I hear my name called. I stare in panic when I spot Harry walking my way with his dog in tow. "Is the head any better?" He beams, kissing me on the cheek. I glance at Grim, who's busy with Oakley and hasn't noticed.

"Yes, much better."

"Do you want to get brunch?"

I shake my head. "Actually, I'm here with Oakley and . . . my friend."

"Oh," he looks around the busy park, "okay. Maybe later?" I nod eagerly, hoping he'll leave before Grim spots him. "I was thinking maybe you could come for dinner one night this week and stay over. We could get a movie?" It's the first time he's invited me to his place.

"I shouldn't leave Oakley overnight," I begin.

"You could leave her with her father," comes Grim's voice, and I cringe with embarrassment.

Harry smiles, holding out his hand. Grim stares at it blankly until he retracts it. "I'm Harry."

"Grim."

"Right. I'm," he smiles at me before shrugging, "seeing Hadley."

"Nice. I'm fucking Hadley," says Grim coldly, and my eyes widen in shock. Harry looks at me for an explanation.

"That's not true," I say quickly.

"Don't you recognise me?" Grim continues. "You took my driving licence from me."

Harry looks uncomfortable. "You do look familiar."

"I am so sorry about this," I say, my cheeks burning with humiliation. "This is Oakley's dad. He's recently come into her life again. We're definitely not a thing anymore, and I promise I'll explain everything later."

"She's got a kid with a criminal," says Grim. "How's that look for you being a judge?"

"In fact, maybe we can grab brunch now," I say, moving towards Harry, who looks confused.

Grim grabs my arm. "I don't think that's a good idea, Hads."

"Stop," I hiss.

"See, I'm her ol' man, and now I'm out of prison and back in her life, I plan on keeping her. So, you're wasting your time if you think you'll win this because she's always loved me, since she was a kid. Ain't that right, Hads?"

"Call me," says Harry, his expression blank. "We'll talk." Then he walks off without looking back.

"He won't answer your calls," says Grim.

"Yes, I realise that, thanks to you!"

"The judge, Hadley, really?"

"He's perfect. He's honest, kind, patient, and above all, a nice guy. He wouldn't sleep with my sister, or anyone else for that matter," I snap.

Grim gets in my face again, and Oakley strokes my cheek. "But could he fuck you like I do?" he whispers in my ear. "Could he make you scream his name?"

"Yes," I snap, turning away from him and sitting back on the bench.

Grim stares at me for a long minute before taking Oakley over to the baby swings.

CHAPTER TWENTY

GRIM

I let a few days pass without bothering Hadley. Since her comment at the park, I've felt angry. I have no right to be, but I can't help it. The thought of her with someone else kills me inside. Deep down, I don't believe she's serious about the judge, cos if she was, she'd have told everyone.

She comes home from work, and I'm in the kitchen trying Oakley on some new food Mama B whizzed up. Hadley recently began weaning her and it's my favourite part of the day. She kisses Oakley on the head and makes a fuss. I love her, and it's these moments that make me regret every fucking bad decision I ever made. "You're a great mum," I blurt out, and she smiles awkwardly. "Sorry, I just felt the need to tell you."

"I'm really impressed with how you've taken to fatherhood actually," she admits. "I didn't expect you to be so hands-on. I think she's loved spending time with you while I work."

I grin, happy she's noticed. "Thanks."

"Look at us being adults," she jokes, shrugging her coat off.

"It would be nice to get along like this more often," I say, and she nods in agreement. "I don't want Oakley to grow up seeing us arguing."

"Will you back off trying to involve yourself in my personal life?"

"I'll try."

"I'm Oakley's mum, not your property."

"Okay. Understood."

She nods, looking pleased with our new truce. "Good."

We bathe Oakley together and laugh as she splashes us. I get her dressed for bedtime, and Hadley makes her a bottle and feeds her while I read a story. Then we put her in her cot to sleep. "I guess I'll leave you in peace," I say, hovering over the cot.

"Thanks for helping."

"I love being with her."

"Maybe on Saturday we could do something as a family," she suggests.

I nod eagerly. "I'd love that."

∞

Saturday arrives and we spend the day at the local Sea Life Centre. Oakley watches the fish and makes cooing noises. I spend most of the time watching Hadley, unable to believe I let her go so easily.

I'm cradling Oakley in my arms when a woman approaches. She's been catching my eye the last few times we've passed, and she's waited for Hadley to go to the bathroom before coming over. "I'm sorry, I don't usually make a habit of doing this, but I couldn't help noticing you," she says, blushing. She reaches down and scoops a toddler up in her arms. "This is Kyle. He's two. I'm Chrystal."

"I'm Grim, and this is Oakley. She's eight months old."

She grins. "Nice to meet you both. Are you alone?" She knows I'm not, but I don't make a big deal.

"Today or in life?" I ask.

"Both."

"Today, I'm with Oakley's mum. But we're not together. I'm single." I feel Hadley behind me and turn, forcing an easy smile. "Speak of the devil." Hadley heard my words, I can see it on her face. "Hads, this is Chrystal and Kyle."

"Nice to meet you," she says, offering half a smile.

"Well, I'll let you get on, but take my number. I'd love to meet for a play date sometime." She hands me a card, and I stuff it in my back pocket. I watch her leave, and Hadley takes Oakley from my arms and marches towards the penguin enclosure.

After a few minutes of silence, I can't take it anymore. "Are you mad?"

"Why would I be?" she asks coldly.

"You seem like you are."

"I'd just prefer you to chat up women when you don't have Oakley in your arms."

I laugh. "I wasn't chatting her up, she approached me."

"Just don't do that in front of Oakley."

I shrug. "Okay, sorry."

"She seemed nice," she adds with an expression that says she doesn't think that at all.

"A little forward. I like reserved and quiet."

"You should call her," she says, nodding, and I frown. "Maybe we can go on a double date."

"Hadley, we've just agreed to get along, I don't think we're quite ready for double dates, do you?"

"Yeah, why not? I've moved on, and you should too. Sixteen months is a long time for you to be single, and I heard the club girls saying you keep turning them down. It's not healthy."

I'm angry. I don't want to fucking date anyone else but her, but she seems so keen to push me away. "I told you, I'm your ol' man. I ain't going anywhere until I'm certain we're done."

Hadley looks me in the eye. "I don't know how else I can make it clear."

"I'll make you a deal. Spend a week with me. Fit me in around work and your other commitments, and I'll convince you we still have something. If at the end of it, you still want to see Judge Jerk, I'll step away. I'll even call Chrystal and arrange the double date myself. But give me one week."

She takes a minute to think about it before nodding. "Fine. One week. Starting Monday."

∞

I get back to the club and I'm late for church. Mav glares as I stomp in and drop down in the chair. "I need a plan," I announce.

"I'm glad you could join us," says Mav sarcastically.

"This is important," I snap. "I've made a deal with Hadley. She's agreed to spend the week with me, and

I have to convince her we're still a thing or let her go forever." Mav groans, and a few of the guys laugh.

"Never gonna happen," says Ghost.

"It would be nice if you could support me on this!"

"I'm being honest, brother. She's happy, leave her be."

I shake my head. "She's the mother of my kid and she isn't going anywhere unless it's with me. So, are you gonna help me or not?"

"Hate to break your bubble, Romeo, but Hadley hates you. It's not gonna happen," says Mav.

I look around the table at the doubting faces of my brothers. "Guys, I need you. Without her, it's pointless. I can't watch her with someone else, raising my daughter, being happy and shit. She's mine. She was made for me, and I love her." They exchange doubtful looks.

Copper slaps me on the back. "Yah know what, a brother in need will always get help from me. Of course, we'll help. What do you need us to do?"

HADLEY

Monday evening, I step from my office and find Grim waiting for me outside. I wrap my coat around me tightly. It's getting to autumn, my favourite time of the year. Grim hooks his arm out, and I take it hesitantly. Touching him makes me weaker, especially when he smells so good, like now.

We walk in the direction of the river, and I spot a man in barista attire with a cart. He smiles as we approach and points to a table nearby. People are going about their everyday business, looking curiously as we take a seat. "I know how much you love coffee, so I contacted my friend here," says Grim, pointing to the man who is now opening up his trolley and taking out small paper cups. "He has a coffee shop that imports coffees from all over the world and he's agreed to share some of his best ones with us."

I can't hide my smile. Coffee is my second love after Oakley, and though Grim isn't as keen, the fact he's here, trying it with me, makes it special.

"Tell me about the early days with Oakley," he says, sipping the first coffee and wincing at the bitter taste. I laugh cos it's strong and perfect for me. The barista only pours a small amount in each cup, just enough to taste it.

"It was hard," I admit. "I didn't really know what I was doing, but I wanted to prove I could cope on my own, so I tried to do it all. Mum eventually made me see sense. Once I let everyone help, it got easier."

"Mav told me you didn't use the money I left."

"I didn't need to. Put it in savings for Oakley to have when she's older."

"What did you do with the letters I sent?"

"I saved them."

"Why?"

"Because maybe I'll read them one day. I read your letters to Oakley at bedtime."

He smiles. "I appreciate that. I went to parenting classes and the tutor suggested it." It impresses me he went to such lengths. "Do you think you'll have more kids?"

"I haven't given it much thought."

"I want more. Maybe this time I could stick around for the birth," he jokes, and we try more coffee. "Okay, so, I have this book on good authority," he says, holding up a paperback. "Each night, I thought we could read a chapter."

He stands, offering me a blanket. I take it and follow him to a nearby tree, where he sits on the ground, pulling me down beside him. "You're gonna read to me?" I ask, arching a doubtful brow.

"You once told me I should read this stuff and maybe I'd learn something, so here we are, learning."

I sip coffee and listen to the beginning of a recent best-selling kinky book. I don't have the heart to tell him I've read it because he seems so determined to share my love of reading. After the first chapter's read, we end the night with a walk through the park before heading back home.

He stops me outside the club. "I had a great time tonight. Thank you for letting me take you out."

"Do you wanna bathe Oakley?" I ask. He smiles, nodding and following me inside.

∞

When Oakley is asleep, Grim goes to his room, and I head downstairs. Meli catches my eye, so I join her on the couch. "How's things?" she asks.

We don't often talk, not properly, just in passing or when she asks about Oakley. "Good. You?"

She nods. "Good. I got a modelling job," she says, and I smile, happy she's finally found something she enjoys doing. "Is Grim helping you out with Oakley?"

My smile fades. This should be a conversation I can share with my sister, but I feel myself pulling away. "Yeah, he's good with her," I mutter.

"I'm glad. You both have the best daughter."

I nod. "We do."

"Can I say one thing?" she asks. I agree reluctantly. "He's not a bad person. He messed up because he was scared of losing the one thing he loved. He's a good dad, and let's face it, we never thought we'd see the day he'd settle down with a kid, but he's rocking it. And you love him, Hads. It's so bloody obvious. You're right to make him work for it, but don't keep him begging too long. He might get bored, and I really want to see you guys make it. You deserve happiness, you both do." She gets up and leaves, and I stare after her, gobsmacked.

CHAPTER TWENTY-ONE

GRIM

Our second date is to the coffee shop she loves the most. We sit in silence, enjoying the ambience of the place. Eventually, we talk about past times we've shared, laughing at some of the stupid things we once did. "Do you think Oakley will stay in the club?" she asks.

"I hope so. It would be nice to see the next generation grow up in the club."

"What if she marries a biker?"

I shudder, and she laughs. "Can we just concentrate on getting her to her first birthday?"

"Meli wants to organise a party," she says. It's the first time she's mentioned her sister to me. "I don't have time, and I guess it wouldn't hurt to let her help."

"Good idea," I say. "Set a budget and I'll cover it."

We take a slow walk back to the club, and once Oakley is in bed, I sit on Hadley's chair in her room while she lies on the bed and I read chapter two in the book. I don't see the hype, but she seems to like it and that's all that matters.

Afterwards, I head downstairs to the kitchen where I find Meli alone, making tea. She looks up just as I'm about to leave. "Don't go," she says.

"Look, I don't think it's a good idea to be caught alone in a room with you."

"I just wanna talk."

"I'm working my arse off to win Hads back, and I don't want her to catch us talking and think we're up to no good."

"Relax. Stay over there, if it means so much to you. I just wanna say, I hope things aren't weird for us. It was in the past and I've moved on. I hope you can forgive me for any trouble I caused."

"Meli, you didn't cause trouble. It was my fault. All of it. I should have owned up straight away and made it clear we'd been together. I was selfish, thinking about what I wanted and not what mattered. I hate myself for ripping you two apart, but in time, I hope I can bring you back together."

The door opens and Hadley steps in. My heart drops, and Meli winces. But Hadley breezes in holding a notepad. "Right, should we make a start on this birthday party?" she asks, sitting at the table and waiting for us both to join her. I exchange a relieved look with Meli. It feels like progress.

Wednesday's date is at the bar I always go to when I need time alone. It was the first place I shared with her when we were starting to spend time together. It was also the place she watched me get arrested sixteen months ago, and so I'm nervous as to how this date will play out.

Inside, it hasn't changed. We share a smirk as I order our drinks. It's the same faces still here enjoying the silence. Even the barman is the same. As we sit down, I look around and take in the stale air and the dirty carpets and see the place for what it is—a rundown local with depression oozing from its walls. "I don't know why I ever liked it here," I begin. "Looking back, it suited my mood, but these days, I'm a little more upbeat."

She nods. "I notice that about you."

"Oakley gives me reason to keep going," I admit. "I was in a dark place before and I don't even know why. A combination of feeling trapped at the club and facing shit with Mum, I guess. And maybe the stress of doing what I did with Meli . . ." I trail off, watching for her reaction. "I knew it was wrong."

"I heard you last night," she confesses, "talking to Meli."
"Right."
"You were the first man to hurt me, to break my heart so completely and utterly, that it's taken me this long to begin to heal. But holding on to all the anger and hurt is tiring. Meli has moved on, probably several times." We both laugh. "And we have a daughter. So, for her sake, I forgive you. I understand why you lied about it, that it wasn't to intentionally hurt me but because you were scared of losing me. I get that now."

I feel the weight of guilt lifting from my shoulders. "Thank you, that means so much to me."

"Last time we were here, you were saying goodbye."
"Seems like forever since then."
"What was it like, being inside?"

I laugh. "Awful. If I thought the club was a cage, it was nothing compared to prison. It gets easier the more times you go, though."

She smiles. "Well, don't make a habit of it. I didn't like Oakley having to visit her daddy there."

"She was a hit with the inmates. They loved her."

"Cambridge stuck to his word," she says. "He left Harriett and Ivy alone. She's got a nice place in central London, and she's opening a boutique selling children's clothes. She's doing really well."

"That's a great outcome for her and a success story for the club. It's good knowing we can help these women get back on their feet."

"I think Ghost misses her. Nothing happened between them, but I think he secretly liked her."

Right on time, the door opens, and Ghost comes in with a huge bunch of red roses. He makes a show of approaching the other tables and repeating the same line in broken English that the rose seller did to us all those months ago. "You buy rose?"

After a few of the men blank him, he makes his way to us and smiles. "Aww, a beautiful lady need beautiful rose."

Hadley laughs. "What are you doing?"

"You buy rose?" he asks, looking at me.

I roll my eyes. He's taking his role far too seriously as I dip into my pocket and pull out my wallet. "I'll take the lot," I say.

"Good. After what you did, she deserves so much more. A house, maybe a dog . . . a wedding—"

"Enough," I say, cutting him off. Hadley laughs harder.

"You a piece of shit, you have lot of making up to do. Roses don't mean she give you fucky fuck."

"Ghost, you've made your point," I mutter.

He reaches into my open wallet and takes some cash out. "Arsehole," he utters, folding at least fifty in notes and stuffing them in his pocket.

"You're an arsehole. Next time, I'll let Scar do it. He's less of a talker," I say, snatching the roses and handing them to Hadley. He swoops down and kisses Hadley on the cheek before making his exit. "Sorry, he got a little over-excited in his role," I say.

"Don't be. He was much funnier than the original rose seller. I still have it, by the way, the rose." I grin at her confession. "It's dry and shrivelled, much like our relationship," she says, winking, "but I kept it anyway."

After a couple more drinks, we head back to the club for bathtime with Oakley. Once she's asleep, I take Hadley by the hand and lead her outside. It's weird touching her after not being allowed for so long. I feel like small electric pulses are passing from our hands.

We go outside to the oak tree. Our oak tree.

HADLEY

This feels like our special place. I always felt close to him here, and after he left, I'd cry in this spot. I rub my chest, remembering how much it hurt back then. I thought I'd never get over it, but here we are again, acting like he didn't rip out my heart and stamp all over it. Listening to him talking with Meli last night, I realised just how much I've missed them both being in my life. I came to the conclusion that they miss me just as much, so what is keeping us apart, except for me being stubborn? They can't change the past, but I can change our future. Oakley needs them both in her life and so do I.

Grim tugs me to sit beside him, then he throws a blanket over us both and opens the book. This time, he continues to read more than one chapter. Snuggled under the blanket, listening to his rumbling voice has me rooted to the spot, and after some time, I lay my head against his shoulder and close my eyes. I feel like I'm home.

CHAPTER TWENTY-TWO

GRIM

The following day, I feel stressed. "It's not working," I say, pacing Mav's office. Rylee gives me a sympathetic look. "She would have said something to you, and she hasn't, which means she isn't impressed or swayed," I continue.

"I could go ask her how she's getting on," Rylee suggests.

"I don't want you to dig. If she was thinking about taking me back, she'd have told you. I know she would have."

"Hadley's kind of distanced herself from me. Not in a bad way, just she's busy with work and Oakley. We don't talk like we used to."

"I need something bigger, better."

"You revisited past dates, you've done shit she loves . . . how about you make new memories," Mav suggests.

"Like?"

"I don't know, use your imagination. Surely, you can think of a date."

It took a lot of organising and begging, mainly because the woman in charge was stricter than fucking Hitler. But I cracked her, and now, I'm waiting by a candlelit table—fake candles because of Hitler. I feel nervous. This feels like the make-or-break date. Thursday already and I'm here wondering what kind of fucking pussy organises a dinner date in a library that apparently survived the second World War.

Mav leads Hadley in, her arm hooked in his. She looks around in awe and it's the effect I was hoping to have as her eyes land on me. "Does Betty Battle-axe know about this?" she asks, smiling wide.

"If you mean Hitler, yes, she knows. I'm lucky to have survived with my balls still attached."

She giggles and the sound almost takes my breath away. Mav kisses her on the cheek before stepping out and leaving us alone. "It looks beautiful."

"As do you," I say, pulling out the chair for her to sit.

I lift the lid on our dinner, and she laughs at the discovery of burgers underneath. "In my defence, I only had a short window and Hitler was very specific about the use of heat and flame, so having a chef cook right in front of us was a definite rule-breaker."

She smiles even wider. "This is perfect, Grim. Really perfect."

I take my seat. "The library is full of secrets. Books that hold a world of them." I pour us each a glass of water. "So, here goes. The first girl I ever kissed was when I was six years old. Janey Peaches. She smelt funny and I'm pretty sure she'd been eating sand right before I planted my lips on hers as a dare. Your brother's dare, might I add. Anyway, she punched me right in the face and told me she was gonna tell her dad. I wasn't scared cos I knew I could take her dad, even at six years old. My first time was with Erica Bradshaw. I was ten, and she was thirteen. She was a crazy motherfucker and into some weird shit for a kid. I was scared after that for months."

I laugh to myself, lost in the memories of my childhood. "Jenifer Wood. She was second. I remember her because right before I met up with her, I'd killed my mum's latest boyfriend. I remember turning up at her house with the confidence of a lion, like I was some big motherfucker afraid of no one. I asked her out because rumour had it she was easy, and I needed easy in my life seeing as everything else was so fucking hard. She didn't want to have sex, but I was pumped from what I'd done earlier, and I talked her into it. I felt like a prick after. After that, women became faceless. I can't tell you names, ages . . . I can't even picture them. I can tell you places, maybe . . . an alleyway, a club parking lot, the cinema, a bar. So many places. And then I noticed Meli."

Hadley shifts uncomfortably, but it needs to be said so she can understand everything.

HADLEY

I hold my breath, preparing for his confession of undying love for my twin. I'm not sure I can handle the truth, but something tells me I need to hear it, so I sit quietly, waiting for him to continue. "She reminded me of Janey Peaches," he smirks, "and that reminded me of times when I felt innocent. When I wasn't soiled with blood and guilt and women's cheap perfume. When it was all about funny smells and sand grains on lips.

"Meli didn't give a crap about offending people or sticking to rules. I never told her how I felt, just watched from a distance and wondered what it would be like to be so guilt-free and happy. I didn't know the truth then, that she felt just as soiled and used as me. The night Rosey returned and everything came out, I was floored. Like we all were. And when everyone had gone to bed, and I was alone with my bottle of Jack, I sat behind the bar and cried.

"I didn't see it, even though I watched her, so I blamed myself. And on top of that, I felt guilty for being jealous over her carefree life when in actual fact she was suffering worse than I ever did. She found me behind the bar, and we drank. We drank so much, I don't even know how we ended up doing what we did. And I can't sit here and lie, I can't tell you I woke up and regretted it, because I didn't. But I didn't remember it either. It was just like all the other times, yet she wasn't faceless. She was Meli, the woman I'd been pining after for years.

"The second time, I was drunk again, but I knew what I was doing. I wanted a second chance to remember what I didn't from the first. That time, I regretted it. It felt wrong. So, I had a small pity party, torn over whether I should walk away from the club and stay the hell away from my President's little sister or stay and get lured in over and over because I knew I wouldn't turn her down if she came to me again.

"Then you started appearing. When I felt like shit, there you were to cheer me up. If I'd had a bad day, you came along and sat with me until I felt better. Sitting under that damn tree became my favourite thing to do. Sometimes, I sat there waiting for you, then you wouldn't show and

I'd be pissed. I'd have to go for a ride to stop myself from stalking you and forcing you to sit with me. You made my dark days light again. You're the first woman to do that."

I sip my water and push my half-eaten burger away. My heart aches at his confessions, and for the first time in a long time, I want to wrap him in my arms and tell him it will be okay. Somehow, we'll work it all out. I purposely put myself on his radar. I decided I wanted him, and I put myself under his nose so he'd take notice. Did I give him a choice? If I hadn't done that, if I'd have just stayed in my lane, maybe we wouldn't be here now, both suffering.

"You were the first woman to get my attention without getting naked. You intrigued me and woke me up. You challenged me without being confrontational and made me stop and think about my actions. Being around you was like having a life lesson." He laughs. "You even made shopping fun." I nod, grinning. "That was a big day for us both."

"When we slept together, I didn't think about Meli or the shit I should bring to your attention. I didn't think about the consequences of falling in love with you way before we had sex, but once we'd done that too, there was no going back. I was in too deep.

You were the whole package, and there was no way I was gonna risk losing you and throwing myself back into the dark. I guess what I want you to understand is, I once thought I loved Meli, but I didn't. I was infatuated with the idea of being carefree and happy. I thought having Meli meant I would be like that. Turns out, to feel those things, I needed to actually be happy.

"You make me happy, Hadley. You have no idea how amazing you are and how amazing you make me. I love you. I have loved you from the minute you forced me to take you clothes shopping. I will never understand what I put you through, but I know you can't just get over it and move on, cos it was huge. I've arranged for you to go on the date tomorrow with Harry." My eyes widen and my heart stutters in my chest. "I couldn't bring myself to do the whole double date thing, but I've booked and paid for a table at Loratz."

Loratz is exclusive and costs a lot of money. My brain is yelling for me to tell him I don't want to go there with Harry. But Grim reaches across the table and holds my hands in his.

"Go on the date. Enjoy his company. You'll know if he's right cos you'll enjoy the night and never want it to end, just like I don't want this one to end. And after, if you find yourself leaning in to kiss him, you'll know I'm well and truly in your past and you've moved on."

"I've never kissed him," I say. "I just wanted you to think that."

He smiles, winking. "I know when you're lying, Hads. And I knew you hadn't slept with the jackass judge." I smile. "But you need to make sure, cos if you come home and tell me you're finished with him, I'll be making you mine forever. I'm not giving you another chance to get away from me."

Grim stands, holding out his hand. I take it, and he leads me to the stairs. We walk around the library together. He lets me look at the hundreds of dusty books, but all I can think about is his words and how I wish he'd push me up against these books and kiss the life out of me. I don't want to date Harry, I already know that, but I know he's going to make me go on the date regardless so I can reassure him I'm his.

We're late back to the club tonight, and Mum has already put Oakley to bed. Grim leads me out to the oak tree for the second night running so he can read the book to me. "I chose her name because of the tree," I say quietly.

He kisses me on my temple. "I know."

CHAPTER TWENTY-THREE

HADLEY

Smoothing the dress, I stare at myself in the mirror. Why does it feel like I'm doing something wrong? The bedroom door opens and Grim steps inside with Oakley in his arms. He stops dead, and a look of regret passes over his face. "You okay?" I ask.

He nods, looking anything but okay. "Doesn't Mummy look amazing?" he whispers to Oakley, who babbles in response.

"Are you sure you're okay looking after her?" I repeat, making conversation to stop the awkwardness. He nods again. "Look, I can cancel this—"

"No. You need to do this. I'm fine. Have a good night. We'll talk tomorrow." He disappears into the bathroom to run Oakley's bath.

∞

I take a breath to steady my nerves before going inside the restaurant. It's breathtaking inside, all sparkles and chandeliers. I spot Harry at a table, and he waves me over. He stands to pull out my chair, and I'm reminded of Grim doing the same thing last night.

"I must say, I've never been asked on a date by a woman's ex before," he says, smiling. "I was most surprised."

"Me too," I mutter.

"So, what is this? A trial? A way of your ex telling you he's moving on?"

I shake my head. "A final decision."

"Well, if he's paying, we may as well make the most of it."

The waiter comes over to take our order, and Harry asks for champagne. "I can recommend the chicken salad," he tells me, so I smile at the waiter and order that. Harry then orders duck, and I suddenly feel insulted that he pushed me to have salad.

While we wait for food, he tells me about his day, but I find my mind going to Grim and Oakley, wondering if they're sleeping now or if he's telling her another story.

Our food comes, and I pick at the salad while Harry tells me about his holiday recommendations. He asks me if I've ever been to the South of France, and I want to laugh as I shake my head. A moment of clarity hits me—how would Harry ever fit into the club? He wouldn't. I couldn't invite him for dinner without one of the guys interrupting or a play fight breaking out in the main room. He'd hate the way Ghost pulls my hair and kisses me every time he passes me, or the way the men steal my daughter for cuddles. In Harry's world, it's clean and clear. We'd be a family in a lovely house who holiday in France. My world is less glamorous. It's loud and chaotic, crazy and full of drama, but I love it. It's all I've ever known.

"This was a bad idea," I tell him, pushing my arms into my jacket.

He looks surprised. "It was?"

"I'm so sorry, Harry. You're a really nice guy," albeit a little self-obsessed, but still . . . "but you're not for me. Have dessert. I can make my own way back." I rush from the restaurant before he can protest and flag down a cab.

The main room is still busy when I get back, and I spot Grim at the bar with Mav. I grab his hand, and he looks surprised to see me. "We have somewhere to be," I say, tugging him away from Mav and outside.

"Are you okay? How was the date?"

I lead him towards the oak tree, stopping under its wiry branches and turning to face him. "I had sex once before you with a guy who spent the first years of school bullying me. I think I did it because I wanted him to leave me alone, but I hated it, every second of it. It didn't work either because he just bullied me more." I shake my head, frowning at my rambling state.

"I can't tell you stories of my first kiss or my first in anything because you are my first, Grim. My first real kiss, my first real date, my first love, my first heartbreak. The truth is, I don't need a date to tell me who I want or who makes me happy. It's you, Grim. It's always been you, and even when I thought I'd die from heartache, I still wanted you to hold me and make it better. You gave me Oakley—how can I ever love anyone as much as I love you and her?"

He steps closer, running a hand through my hair and smiling down at me, his eyes full of love. "You didn't like the date?"

"The restaurant was beautiful, the company not so much. Give me a burger and a biker any day," I say with a wide smile.

"You realise what you're agreeing to, right?"

"Remind me."

"This is it. No one else. Just me and you forever. You're mine and I'm yours, and no one is coming between us."

"I think I can handle that."

"If you can't, you have less than a second to step away cos when my lips hit yours, that's it, you've sealed your fate." His lips are inches away.

"Like a contract?" I whisper.

Cupping my face in his hands, he presses his lips against mine, and I feel explosions in my stomach. I've waited so long for this moment and didn't even know it. "Like a contract," he confirms, pulling back slightly. "I love you, Hadley. Forever."

"I love you too, Hudson. Forever."

THE END

Ghost - The Perished Riders MC

Take a look at what's next...
Chapter One
NELLY

"I need help," I tell Rylee, flopping onto the couch beside the President's ol' lady.

She closes the book she's reading and turns sideways to face me. "Okay, who am I killing?" she asks, her expression serious. I smile. She doesn't even know what I need, yet she's happy to help. We've been friends for a couple of years, ever since I helped her leave her abusive ex-husband with the help of The Perished Riders MC.

"You can keep your knife in its case," I joke. "It's not that kind of help. My parents are in London for a few weeks sorting out some business, and I need to show them I have my life together here."

Rylee frowns. "Don't you have your life together?" I scoff. "Yes, did I forget to introduce you to my wealthy husband who owns a beautiful house in Sandringham?"

"Nelly, they're your parents, why do they care if you're single? Being in a relationship doesn't mean you have your life together."

I roll my eyes. "You don't know them." I sigh, feeling like a bitch. "They mean well and they're great, honestly, but they think I'm settled with a good job and a wonderful fiancé."

"You've lied to them already?"

I nod, shame washing over me. "Mum was always setting me up on dates, and I got sick of it. When I met my ex, she backed off, so I didn't tell her we'd split up."

"So, you want a fake boyfriend?" she asks, laughing.

"I know, it sounds crazy, but it's just for a few weeks. Then they'll go home, and I probably won't see them again for another six months."

"I don't know any men who your parents might approve of," says Rylee. "We could ask Arthur if he knows someone. Or maybe one of his brothers could help you out?"

I screw my face up in a way that tells her I'm not a fan of that idea. Arthur Taylor and his brothers are big time London gangsters. If I ask them for a favour, I'll have to repay them, and Lord only knows what they'd want from me. "I was kind of thinking of one of the guys here," I suggest, looking around the mc club.

"You want a biker to pretend to be decent?" she jokes. She looks around the clubhouse too before shrugging. "Okay, well, just go ask someone."

"They're more likely to do it if the Pres's ol' lady was to ask." I smile sweetly, and she groans. "Please, I wouldn't ask if I wasn't desperate. It's a couple of dinner dates at most. I'll even pay."

"I guess free food might entice them." Rylee looks around again. It's always busy in the evenings, which is why I love this shift the best. I've been working the bar at the clubhouse for a few years, ever since I pushed my way in here and convinced Maverick he needed me. It was supposed to be temporary to help me out with cash after my relationship broke down. But I love it so much, I can't face leaving. "What about Michael?"

"The vicar?" I almost screech, and a few of the guys look our way. I lower my voice. "I can't ask a man of the church to lie for me."

"Good point. Dice?" I shake my head. "No, he stresses me out with his weird behaviour and the way he rolls the dice to make every damn decision. I can't imagine my parents would be impressed with him rolling sixes to decide what dinner he wants."

Rylee laughs. "Tatts or Ghost then?"

I consider the pros and cons quickly in my head. "Tatts," I decide. He's a typical guy who never seems to have a girlfriend and prefers drinking with his brothers over dating. I think my parents could overlook the tattoos, and Mum would fall for his cheeky laddish banter.

Rylee shouts him over. "We need your help."

He eyes us suspiciously. "Is it gonna get me hurt by the Pres?"

"It's more for Nelly than me," Rylee explains. "She needs a date."

His eyes fall to me, and he narrows them suspiciously. "You wanna date me?"

"Not for real. It's an act to get my parents off my back. They're in town for a few weeks, so it'll be a three-week max kind of deal."

He screws his nose up. "I don't really do parents. The last girl I dated took me to meet her olds and they moved to another country two days later, taking her with them.

I'm not the sort of man that dads like their daughters to date."

"Can't you just act for a couple of nights?" asks Rylee.

"It depends. What do I get out of it?"

"The knowledge you helped Nelly out of a tight spot."

Maverick joins us, placing a kiss on Rylee's head. They're so sweet together, I find myself watching them closely with envy. They give singletons like me couple goals that I'll probably never achieve. "What's going on?" he asks.

"Nelly wants a fake boyfriend for a couple dates over the next few weeks," Rylee explains. "I'm trying to convince Tatts that he would make the ideal man for the job."

Mav sniggers. "You know he scares parents to move their daughters to other countries. You'd be better with someone responsible, like Ghost."

"Yes, Ghost. He's way better at charming people," agrees Tatts before making his escape.

I glance over to where Ghost is sipping his bottle of beer. Out of all the guys, we don't speak much. I get the impression he doesn't like me, and he scowls an awful lot whenever I try to make conversation with him. Rylee waves him over, but he hesitates before joining us. "We need your help," says Rylee. "Nelly needs someone to pretend to date her for the next few weeks."

"No," he says firmly before walking away again.

"Brother," snaps Mav, and Ghost groans before returning and forcing a tight smile for his President. "Don't disrespect my ol' lady like that," he warns.

"Sorry, Pres. I didn't mean to. I just don't wanna get involved in whatever girl drama this is," he explains.

"She just needs someone to accompany her to a few dinners," says Rylee.

"It's fine. Don't worry about it, I'll sort it myself," I mutter, feeling my face burn with embarrassment. I didn't want to make such a big thing about it, and now I feel like everyone is listening in.

"What the fuck else are you gonna do?" Mav asks Ghost. "You're not on any jobs for me, so you're free."

"I just don't wanna pretend to date Nelly," Ghost snaps.

"Yah know, your attitude lately is shit. First, you disrespect my ol' lady by walking away when she's still talking to you, and now you're snapping at me?"

"Honestly, it's fine. It's not a big deal," I mutter.

"Nelly looks after us. She pulls all the hours she can, and she needs the club's help," Mav continues like I haven't spoken. "So, why won't you help her out?"

Ghost looks irritated. "Is it a club problem?"

"It is now, I'm making it club business. Make yourself free for whenever Nelly needs you. Is that clear?" asks Mav.

"Crystal, Pres," mutters Ghost through gritted teeth.

Mav grins and stands, pulling Rylee with him. "Great. We'll leave you to discuss the details. Nelly, if he messes up, tell me." They walk away hand in hand, and I sit awkwardly, hoping the ground will swallow me whole.

"I'm really sorry, Ghost. I wanted Tatts to do it. Let's just forget all about it. I'll tell Mav I sorted it."

He scoffs. "I'm the second choice?"

My face burns. "No. Mav said you'd be better at it."

"He's right. Don't choose a boy to be a man. And that's what you want, right? A man to show your parents you're doing good in life?" He looks amused, and I feel like he's laughing at me. "What lies do you need me to spout?"

I knot my fingers together the way I always do when I'm embarrassed or nervous. I don't know why I feel like this when usually I'd tell him to fuck himself. "There's a dinner at my uncle's house tomorrow. I'll introduce you to my parents there. We won't stay for dinner. I'll get us out of it. Just an appearance will be fine."

He shakes his head. "Nuh-uh. If you've got me embroiled in this, we're going all the way. I've got a quick thing with Star," he says, checking his watch. "I'll be back before you finish your shift at eleven." He heads for the stairs, and I watch after him. How does he know when my shift ends?

GHOST

I bury my nose into Star's hair, pushing deeper into her. She fists the sheets, groaning with pleasure. Out of all the club girls, she's the one I have the best time with. And lately, seeing everyone around me settling down has me visiting her way more than I should. Since Mav returned as President, he's had this aim to get the brothers to settle down. He wants the club to feel like a family again, and apparently, filling the place with ol' ladies and kids is the way forward.

I get it. Back in the day, even with his dad, Eagle, as leader, it felt good to be part of the club. Mav, Grim, Scar, and I grew up together in the club, and now that we're patched members, we want that tradition to continue. Except I don't ever meet that one woman who can hold my attention. Women these days are worse than men when it comes to hooking up, and then trying to find someone who tolerates the club life over everything else, just makes my search harder.

I close my eyes, moving slow and deep while picturing Harriett. She was a another one that got away. After the club helped her escape her abusive husband, we got close, though not close enough for my liking. But she was never ready for more, and now, she's moved on from the club to start her life again. She wants friendship, and who can blame her after everything she's been through.

I grip a handful of Star's hair and speed up, slamming hard against her arse and chasing the release I so badly need. Her pussy clenches my cock, and she cries out, shuddering beneath me and soaking the bed sheets with her orgasm. I feel the warmth, and it sends me spiralling with her, growling as I empty into the condom. "Fuck," I mutter, dropping down beside her. She gives me a sexy grin and tucks herself into my side.

"Did anyone ever tell you, you're hot?" she asks, placing gentle kisses over my chest.

I tangle my fingers through her hair. "I gotta go," I whisper, feeling her body sag with disappointment. "Pres has me doing Nelly a favour," I add. "I need to speak to her before she leaves."

"What kind of favour?" Star asks, running her fingers over one of the many tattoos I have on my arm.

"Club business," I say, sitting up. I remove the condom and knot it before grabbing a tissue to wrap it up. I pull up my jeans and stuff it in my pocket. I don't wanna get caught out by a club girl—give them a full condom and a pin and I'll have an unwanted ol' lady with a kid I never asked for. "I'll check in tomorrow."

"Maybe I'll be busy," she mutters, wrapping her sheet around her naked body. I shrug. She's trying to get a reaction, but she knows I don't share, so if she goes to another brother, I won't visit her again. That's the deal we made.

I head back to my room where I dispose of the condom and take a shower. I get downstairs at exactly eleven, and Nelly is just pulling on her coat. I don't know much about her. The other brothers love her, but I don't see the fascination. Sure, she's pretty and maybe a little curvier than I'd usually go for, but she's always made it clear she's not the kind of girl you can mess around with. And these days, she's good friends with all the ol' ladies, so you upset one, you upset them all, and that's not a situation a brother needs to be in.

I hold up my bike keys. "I'll take you home." She blushes. I've never seen it before, but every time I've spoken to her tonight, she's reacted the same. I never had her down for shy.

Outside, I throw my leg over my bike and pass her the spare helmet. She puts it on and climbs on behind me. Her hands go to the sissy bar and, for some reason, I place my hands behind each of her knees and tug her closer until she's practically flush against me. She automatically grabs my kutte to steady herself, and I pull her arms to encircle my waist. Something about having her cling to me feels good, like it's natural. I guess we need to act that way if we're gonna lie to her parents about us.

NELLY
All I can think about the whole ride back to my house is how much I want to grind myself against Ghost. I go

on the back of the guys' bikes all the time, since they often drive me home if I get off work after ten, but I've never felt this kind of heat. Being close to him has awoken something inside of me that none of the other brothers has before. Maybe it's the fact he's never bothered with me. He doesn't ever try it on with me or flirt like some of the other single brothers.

When we stop and I climb off to hand him the helmet, my legs are weak and I'm practically panting. With a shaky hand, I pull out my keys and lead the way up the garden path to my rented house. It's small, but I love having my own space. Mav has offered for me to move into the clubhouse more than once, but I'm not ready to give this up.

I turn on the lights as we pass through the living room and head into the kitchen. "Don't you like the dark?" asks Ghost, smirking.

"Not really," I admit, and his smirk fades when he sees I'm serious. "I once got locked in a cupboard, and since then, I've hated the dark."

He takes a seat at the breakfast bar as I shrug out of my coat. "Nice place."

"Thanks. Look, about tomorrow, I really want to just make a quick appearance to welcome my parents back and then I'll tell them we already have plans for dinner."

"Why are you lying to them?" he asks.

I pull two beers from the fridge and pass him one. "They worry about me. A lot. They're happily married, and they want the same for me. Mum sets me up on dates whenever I'm single."

"What's wrong with that?"

"The men she chooses don't want someone like me," I mutter, embarrassed at having to explain it.

"What's that mean?"

I pluck at my jumper like that explains it. "They want eye candy on their arm." I'm more Netflix and cuddle, not wine bar and socialise. I know women who spend hours getting tans, nails, eyebrows, and lashes, but I'm not that sort of girl. And rich men don't want to take me to galas and lavish functions. And that's alright with me, but it's the sort of man my parents envision me with.

"I'm not gonna give you compliments," he states, and I laugh. "It's not what Mav hired me for."

"I wasn't fishing. I'm just saying that I'm not high maintenance and the men mum sets me up with are looking for that."

"Let's go over what you expect from me," he says, taking a pull from his beer.

"Just go with it. They never met my ex in person, so they don't know anything other than we were engaged."

He almost chokes on the beer. "Engaged?"

I nod. "Yeah. I kind of told them we'd taken the next step because they were getting itchy feet. We'd been together two years before we split up, and I never told them we'd split."

"Your lie is getting out of hand, Nelly. Why don't you just explain you're not together."

"You don't know what they're like," I mutter. "And I'm in too deep now. They're here a few weeks on business and then they'll go home. I won't see them again for months. I can come up with a whole dumping story by then."

"You're not close then?"

I lower my eyes and begin knotting my fingers again. "I just disappoint them a lot."

"Fine. Don't go all puppy eyes on me. I'll do what you need but expect me to pull in a favour of my own occasionally."

I nod, smiling. "Deal."

Continue here …. https://mybook.to/GhostBk4

A note from me to you

The Perished Riders series is my second MC series. If you haven't read the first, go check it out on Amazon, The Kings Reapers MC.

For anything Nicola Jane, head here: https://linktr.ee/NicolaJaneUK

I'm a UK author, based in Nottinghamshire. I live with my husband of many years, our two teenage boys and our four little dogs. I write MC and Mafia romance with plenty of drama and chaos. I also love to read similar books. Before I became a full-time author, I was a teaching assistant working in a primary school.

If you'd like to follow my writing journey, join my readers group on Facebook, the link is above. You can also use that link if you're a book blogger, I'd love you to sign up to my team.

Popular books by Nicola Jane

Riggs' Ruin https://mybook.to/RiggsRuin
Capturing Cree https://mybook.to/CapturingCree
Wrapped in Chains https://mybook.to/WrappedinChains
Saving Blu https://mybook.to/SavingBlu
Riggs' Saviour https://mybook.to/RiggsSaviour
Taming Blade https://mybook.to/TamingBlade
Misleading Lake https://mybook.to/MisleadingLake
Surviving Storm https://mybook.to/SurvivingStorm
Ravens Place https://mybook.to/RavensPlace
Playing Vinn https://mybook.to/PlayingVinn

Other books by Nicola Jane:
The Perished Riders MC
Maverick https://mybook.to/Maverick-Perished
Scar https://mybook.to/Scar-Perished
Grim https://mybook.to/Grim-Perished
Ghost https://mybook.to/GhostBk4
Dice https://mybook.to/DiceBk5

The Hammers MC (Splintered Hearts Series)
Cooper https://mybook.to/CooperSHS
Kain https://mybook.to/Kain
Tanner https://mybook.to/TannerSH

Printed in Dunstable, United Kingdom